Edward Andrew Phillips

The Vision of the Cross and Other Poems

Edward Andrew Phillips

The Vision of the Cross and Other Poems

ISBN/EAN: 9783337252342

Printed in Europe, USA, Canada, Australia, Japan

Cover: Foto ©Andreas Hilbeck / pixelio.de

More available books at **www.hansebooks.com**

THE

VISION OF THE CROSS,

AND

Other Poems.

BY

EDWARD ANDREW PHILLIPS, Esq.

BENGAL ARMY.

LONDON:

HATCHARD & CO. 187 PICCADILLY, W.

1860.

CONTENTS.

iv CONTENTS.

THE VISION OF THE CROSS.

AN ALLEGORICAL POEM.

Earth. The Garden of Childhood. The many paths of Life all lead to the valley of Death. Receiving the Kingdom as a Child. A Flower of the Garden transplanted. Sympathy. The living Way. A Guide to the Hills. Vision of the Cross. The path of Error leads to Unbelief and Despair; Penitence: The Cross in the Storm. The missing Guide is revealed by the light of the Spirit, who leads to the place of Refuge. Resting on the Rock of Ages. The distant Hills.

THE VISION OF THE CROSS.

"And there shall be a tabernacle for a shadow in the day-
time from the heat, and for a place of refuge, and for a covert
from storm and from rain."—*Isa.* iv. 6.

I OVERLOOKED a plain, extending wide,

As meets the eye of mariner, when morn

Struggling with night o'erruffles all the sea

With soft forerunning breeze, to break the mist

And clear a pathway for his tender light.

Faint, far, on every side a landscape dim,

Yet dimly beautiful, for fancy kind

Filled up the want of half-discernment fair,

As ever wont, with touches all her own;

Well shaped each tree, and every glimmering field

Thick stored with bounty, and herself surprised,

Half dreading clearer view which might distract

Enraptured sense, and harsher truths display.

Wider and wider ne'ertheless it grew,

In pleasant robes of varying light adorned,

Smiling from slumber fresh with heavenly dews.

Wild flowers as burst the sudden morn from far

Delighted blushed through all the silver mist

That veiled their beauty from the fervent light,

Trembling 'twixt fields and sky. Where first the Morn

Broke on the twilight stretched a shining chain

Of lofty hills, in mantling lustre robed,

And, stretching thence his glowing arms, he held

The purpled plain beneath in warm embrace.

Ten thousand orisons shook all the woods

With choral music, and from whispering dell

Wild echo challenged, and each stony rock

Moved to soft rapture with the general song,

Till filled the vault of smiling heaven with light,

And grateful Earth with rich harmonious praise.
Then first appear'd no more a plain my view,
Here verdant heights and bare, with steep descents,
And there deep dingles, ran through all its reach,
And forests smooth or broken mixed between
In mingled order, from its centre far
To small perspective; all the various views
Of scene familiar gathered, formed in one.

Now I a garden saw, by sparkling brooks
Profusely nourished, nor were noiser floods
Deep driven there, with loud tumultuous flow
To sound discordant, or dismay the charm
Of song sweet swelling from its rustling groves
To every glad retreat; but whispers breathed
From verdant plot, or wayside violet bed,
Snow-white and fragrant more than all beside,
Spoke still contentment, where, with gaudy wings
Of many powders, fanned the feathery shade

The airy butterfly, or sunny sport

Held drone and ladybird and numerous hordes

Of happy insects ; and beneath the arms

Of spreading lime, beside the babbling rill,

Lay snow-white lambs till cooler hours of play.

These, held by narrow bounds, seemed fairer all

Than other prospect given ; among the trees

Thick overarched, one path embowered ran

From midst its beauties to a gate that there

Closed on the wide expanse, without which lay,

Then distant circling, where the aching eye

To trace them failed, paths numberless outbranched,

Whilst arrowlike this centre way was laid,

Strait bound between ; at one strange spot alone,

One hazy mount, (though there direct it led,)

Lost to my vision veiled ; and far beyond

Burst forth again each errant path and this

In clear display, as 'neath an autumn sky

When noon is past, and lengthening falls the shade

On mistless meadow or unvaried moor,

Imbrowned by changes of the ripening year.

All I had seen from diverse prospects drawn

To me, at length,—a far spectator then—

Appeared to form one sunless passage broad

Through the deep bosom of a darksome vale,

Bound of all nearer than the sun-rise hills.

Dense fixèd gloom hung o'er its barren breast,

Where trees of aspect drear their naked boughs

Extended o'er that path, and canopied

Its solemn stillness, thickening with the gloom,

Buried in which at last the whole were lost.

No power had I to penetrate its depths,

But piercing deep in thought, at intervals

Broke the dull roll of waters on my ear,

As in its midst a loosened torrent raved,

Or tempest-tossed with surging billows smote

Its channel sides in strong tempestuous ire.

I shuddered, and exclaimed :—" What wisdom e'er

Would urge the footsteps onward, and so far,
E'en were it prone to yonder radiant hills,
Since further than that vale no road is shown
Upleading there, nor other path is found
(Welcome it were!) which shall not reach its shade?
Say, ye dark fields! oh, leafless bowers, declare!
Are ye not ever green? or, where the Sun
Averted calls away the trembling dawn,
Eternal do ye stand the tomb of Time
And Time's events?" Ere mine was hushed a voice,
Borne from the garden, bid me start and turn,
As light it echoed o'er the laughing meads.

There one did lean upon its gate and gaze
Beyond, as anxious for that freedom wide,
In admiration's longing wonder lost;
But not from him those merry accents rose
Which seemed a moment to disturb and change
His trancelike reverie: amidst the flowers

There strayed a lovely child, upon whose brow,

As sunshine on the streamlet, I beheld

The name of Peace imprinted soft and clear.

Ah, happy one ! thy locks of gold were bright ;

How deep the lustre of thy laughing eyes !

If e'er they wept, their bitterest tears were shed

Like April's early rain, which, as it falls,

Glad sunshine wipes away, and in the sky

Long dwells a deeper and serener blue.

" See," she exclaimed with eager voice again,

" Within this rosy arbour I have found

A volume placed, a shining treasure—see !

On all those paths beyond there cannot be,

My brother, aught so fair, or streams and flowers,

As these around, or beautiful as now

The prospect of yon rising hills from here !"

" Sister," the youth in thoughtless mood replied,

" Why there remain ? the sunshine overhead

To show the splendour of yon spacious fields

Is given : Come, let us, in those valleys white

With daisies of the spring, together roam ;

Or shall I but a little while be gone,

Of every bud that fairest there is found

To twine a wreath to deck my sister's brow ?

Why still so silent ?   Peace, oh, tell me why

Thou car'st for nothing save those hills remote

We cannot reach ? we know not *what* is there."

   Like heavenly music to my ears arose

That babe's soft answer, that, with smile half sad,

To him, whose name was writ Unwise, she gave :—

" Their light is dear, nor there is valley dark

To fright me when I gaze, however far !

And what a beauteous place must that needs be

Whose sunshine tints these leaves and flowers around!

There often do I think can be no night,

For when at early hour the songs awake

And call me from my rest, first there I look,

And all is glorious, and my heart is glad :

Nor when the peaceful sea unrippled shines

Beneath the setting sun, and with the plains

Grows twilight grey, are they too shadow'd o'er,

Most lovely then !   And nightly gilded seen

When hours of sleep arrive ; for, turned on them,

These eyes scarce-willing close, and pictured scenes

Such as are there my happy dreams divide !

But more than all, the only hindrance here

To perfect pleasure is at last removed ;

For this straight path these eyes can now behold

Pass o'er the bosom of yon hazy mount

Above the vale, and to those realms I love :

Oh ! wondrous mount !"—She ceased; a sight ap-
    peared

Of sudden glory strange ; for down that way

Came One exceeding beautiful and bright,

With rainbow splendour, wide-encompassed round,

Of heavenly mildness grand; such form perchance,

A God confessed, where every tribe and tongue

Before the golden image prostrate fell,

At sound of music upon Dura's plain,

The guilty Babylonian monarch awed;

Fourth in the powerless furnace of his pride,

And kindling wrath to Judah's children blest:

Though nought of terrible that aspect mild

Or fear imparted, with uneasy dread,

Unwise shrank back into the neighb'ring shade

Suspicious gazing, as when fallen of old

From lofty innocence to shame defiled,

The sound familiar of his Maker's tread

Bid Adam's heart grow faint, and to the trees

His footsteps hasten with ungrateful speed.

Meanwhile more lovely, but with paler face,

She who had watched him from afar was seen:

Nor once those eyes, grown wat'ry with the light,

Withdrew, nor once those tender hands unclasped.

It seemed the little fair one's heart would burst
With adoration great; and now He came
With outstretched arms, and took her kindly up
Into their bright protection — seemly rest
For beauteous Peace !   From off a rosy bank
Where she had laid it, then the Book he raised,
And beckoning onward from his near retreat
Her frightened brother, in his hand laid down
The costly treasure, cased in burnished gold,
With clasp secured, in which a pearl was set
Of price unreckoned : yet as oft doth change
The object of a dream, transforming slow,
The wond'rous gem a crimson drop became —
The Volume's seal ! from fear to fixed amaze
Grew too his thoughts who held the curious prize,
And sought to open, but the hand that gave
Restrained the effort, and slow bending o'er,
A breath more soft than even's passing sigh
The Bright One breathed, when quick it open flew,

And, to a thousand atoms shaken thus,
The crimson drop fell inward and bedewed
Its every page, which rich inspersion gave
The whole unearthly lustre strange to view.

Unwise methought for ignorance stood dumb;
Not Peace the same; with heavenly wisdom wise,
Clapping her little hands she straight began
A song of Heaven to sing: it could not be
Of Earth, for echoes, faint among the skies,
Were heard, which soon in wilder song burst forth,
Then angels robed in white passed overhead,
And floating downwards joined their anthems all,
Whilst hers grew less distinct, and far away
Died as the music of a dream at dawn!
"Oh, gentle Peace!" her watching brother cried,
"Why hast thou ceased with voice, so welcome e'er,
Of fond affection, aught to me to tell?
Midst all this glory now forget'st thou quite

I love thee still ?   Reach, reach thine hand to me !"
But He who held the precious burden gave
That loved one into angel arms, spread soft
To waft her upward to the longed-for hills,
E'en now less earthly than all pure as they.
From off her face those floating locks of gold
Fell shining back ; and once again she smiled,
Whispering faintly as on high they rose,
" Follow, dear brother, this bright road — Farewell !"
Then o'er the open page his tears fell fast,
And hurried sobs through that fair garden hushed
The usual mirth, and made it solemn all.
He wept for her who might not ask him more
Beside his sister there content to roam,
Who loved it best and all its prospects fair.
" Now," he exclaimed, " I would at once away !
Each flower her hand has touched has lost its bloom ;
And all the streams run mournfully, for ne'er
Her merry laugh shall join their echoes more !"

Thus he bewailed ; and not rebuked or stilled

That outburst vehement by word or gaze

Of Him beside his bending form who stood ;

For, bright beheld beneath that drooping lid,

A tear did rest, which in a while ran down

His radiant cheek and on a blighted rose

Shed its rich moisture, till it bloomed again !

Then turning to the youth he there addressed

Kind words of comfort, and instruction gave

To guard the Book, his future guide, for now

He must his journey to the hills extend

Through unknown scenes, since here He bid him know,

Should storms and tempests, of unsparing wrath,

Far from the setting sun sweep eastward dark,—

Rude desolate the garden's smitten bloom,

And lay the forest's shrinking shelter bare.

Methought he said, " In all this labyrinth

Of paths, but one with safety canst thou tread ;

Within the pages of thy Guide 'tis called
The 'living way,' and there are all declared—
Their names and natures, and their ending one.
Eastward full many a league thou long hast seen
Those mountain heights, where lightsome morning
 first
Lay out his basking pinions on the sky,
Whence light through all the universe has drawn
Its primal essence ; there are mansions there,
And to their adamantine city walls,
Whose streets of gold as glass transparent shine,
Are gates of pearl, there rivulets of life
Pure from its Prince's throne of sapphire roll
In crystal floods, on either verdant side,
Unfading foliage rustles sweet response
To seraph harps refined, and ever tuned
Thro' all the courts of Paradise divine ;
Nor sun by day nor moon's pale beam shall smite
The pilgrim blest that once can enter there.

But since for thee for ever too remote

And inaccessible its rest to gain,

From wrath escaping, there is placed between

A needful shelter, and secure retreat :—

Diverging unto neither hand, pursue

The path of vision ; canst thou thither see

Aught steep ascending, or aloof that soars

In gradual summit through the riven mist

Distinct from all ?"   The rising mount I saw

As thus he spoke : its base was stable rock,

Round which below full many a rudely torn

And straggling shrub, and many a barkless tree,

Betrayed the wreck that former storms had wrought ;

But on the rock and up its bright ascent

No scar appeared, or other boding sign.

O'er all suffused, the selfsame vapour hung

That ever there had disappointed all

My wishful gaze, for on its crest within

Shone grassy greenness and enticing bloom.

"There," said the Bright one, "stedfast now thy gaze

Fix, as thy life is dear!— I go to lift

The cloud that always must conceal that spot

And Heaven's high-road without me ; wait and see."

He ceased, and on my startled trance came down

A heavy darkness, wide revolving o'er

All buried prospect, save one space illumed,

Whence rose a sound as, swifter than their flow,

O'er many waters floats ; for, round His form,

In columns thick rolled back the pond'rous mass,

And, centre of his self-born glory, He

Alone was seen.   Not all that lost beside,

So dimly vanished, brought regret whilst He,

The only fairest, fixed my wand'ring eye ;

But o'er himself the fearful veil at last

Condensed he drew ! then gloomy sounds arose ;

All nature groaned, and seemed to sit in chains

Thro' all the universe that rattling hung,—

A doleful prison ; every pebbly stream

And wailing forest answering, wept unseen;
Could this be that my earliest wonder woke
With sweet surprise, now more to be compared
To realms of fallen spirits and despair?

"Oh, death itself," I heard a voice beneath
Stifled exclaim, "Oh, death itself than this
Were far more welcome! why hast thou,
Most glorious Being, thus withdrawn thy smile
From all around me, and resigned to woe
Spirit and nature?" While he spake the same,
O'er nature wide a glimmering faintly fell,
For, far suspended in the midway air,
A sudden globe of meteor-glory burst,
To a wide halo formed, wild wonders round!
Creation trembled, and, the death-like pause,
Sublime succeeding, from the verge of heaven
Came waves of music rolling thro' the world
Of choirs celestial; what a scene was there!

A man of sorrows, pale and wan with woe
And piteous anguish ! on a cross He hung,
With tight-bound thorns His bleeding temples torn,
Hung on His bosom cold, in bitter death !
All, all alone ! Ah, wherefore sound ye, sweet
Ethereal harpers ? why, so late in tears,
Unfeeling nature, art thou silent now ?
Was sorrow, e'er like His deep sorrow seen,
Whom Heaven hath sore afflicted ? yet thou tun'st,
Seraph of light, some wondrous tale of love
Wiser than mortal, thus thy strains unknown
Flow from the confines of the heavenly world.
Prostrate in terror lay Unwise below,
Yet prostrate tearless, and in dumb dismay ;
When sudden all this mystic vision changed ; —
A silv'ry cloud broke o'er the Crucified,
And, floating thin in flexuous folds away,
The cross stood bare, and, leaning on its side,
Fair majesty serene ! the crown He wore

From brier to myrtle grown of living bloom :
Each hill broke forth in singing, and the trees
Clapped all their hands, and nature smiled again
To see her King from victory restored !
" What meaneth this ?" I asked; " and who is He
So sad, so beautiful, with garments dyed,
Alone who stands, and wears the myrtle crown ?"
Up to the skies His piercèd hand He raised,
And all the distance God-like echoes bore :—
" Weary and heavy laden, come to me
And I will give you rest ! come, ye who thirst,
These waters drink and never thirst again !
No money and no price, oh hungry soul,
To buy the bread of life my blood has bought,
Is needful here ; and that alone shall bid
Thee fear to touch the heavenly feast divine !
And come, thou pilgrim, with no strength, to find
Hell weak and Satan powerless to assail
Thee, mighty, here, and safe from every storm !"

Then methought the bright One, soaring swiftly,

Swept through the fields of space and left revealed

A pathway clear beneath the sheltering cross,—

High o'er the darksome valley to the hills,—

And bright it shone as his white garments spread,

Fused in the sunshine of the eastern skies,

And lost in light unshadowed far beyond.

Now did I mark the footsteps so upheld,

To glorious purpose, as upon his way

Unwise, o'er hill and vale, and often hid

In tangled wood, went on, till far behind

The garden lay, and seemed the cross more near;

Often at first in quiet shade he'd sit,

And search the pages of his guide awhile,

Then thus invigorate his path pursue;

But seldom later, weary and depressed

With toil fatiguing, though, the less he sought

For strengthening there, the tardier he sped.

Close to the living way where first aside

It outward branched, I now a path beheld

Of deadly snare, for all its worst deceit

Was subtle Error to display as truth

And all beside the Book's clear page confuse ;

It passed a desert space beneath the rock,

And lures in fatal treachery so far

The expectant heart to refuge it disdains : —

(So, terrible beneath the placid deep,

To gentle undulation sparkling moved,

Lie couched the barbèd rocks : all fav'ring sweep

The guiltless winds, and swell the spheric sails ;

Proud glides the gallant ship, and hearts of joy,

With thousand different pulsations wild,

Respond the music of the murmuring sea ; —

But hark ! what horror of confusèd cry

Bursts from the smitten planks, and with the crash

Of severed mast, across the pathless main,

Reverberates to the startled skies of noon !)

As cruel path, as prone to dreadful end,

And woe inevitable, this I saw;

And saw with pain the youthful pilgrim haste,

Therein unconscious, and his guide unsought!

Peace, happy Peace! thou didst not bid him there

Thy angel journey follow, with the last

Voice of affection in the garden breathed,

And fond farewell, nor, brighter vision, thou

Bid haste from danger to the cross secure,

So dearly purchased! and are all forgot?

Here many arbours of enticing show

Were round disposed with care in tempting shade,

By all a glassy rill went sparkling clear,

Filling with music low the tuneful groves,—

Delusive brook! the waters of whose flow

Supplied a course perverted from the bed

Of one which ran the straighter road along;

Steps to the cross, and, midway shelter, called,

Were all these bowers, poor screen from tempest bleak

Or cutting torrents, when the floods descend,

And rivers swell, and madness there to rest
Beholding life's eternal refuge nigh.
As wore the noonday stealingly along,
Unwise would gaze, at times, where far behind
His loved companion wandered at his side,
And wish 'twere morn again, thrice happy morn !
And then would doubtful grow as much his wont.

Across his path, when many a weary mile
Erroneous wandered, stretched an opening glade,
His heart reviving : for no future now
Distressed or troubled as his present toil :—
About exhausted to recline him there,
First one coiled serpent startled, then would move
The yellow grass in live commotion all,
And, backward springing, scarce their darts he 'scaped
Whose eyes flashed venom fixed from every tuft
And grassy mound, on him approaching there !
Then terror seized him and he gazed around ;

His way-worn limbs and burning temples bid

Him onward look if nigh the cross he stood,

But dim was that from this unhallow'd glade.

And as to unclose the Book his trembling hand

Sought for its clasp, it weaker shook and failed,

Nor could his eyes find aught whereon to rest,

Unto those gliding serpents in his path

By fascination every moment drawn :

Now here I marked that he, who to destroy,

Had planned this deadly path in days of yore,

Lest one so far enticed, at this dread spot,

Might seek his guide discouraged, had disposed

On either hand a snare ; two spacious bowers ;—

One thickly intertwined and large within,

Dispelled the light of heaven, and on the cross

Turned its dense back ; a cold and subtle den

Of present death and future, stored full well

With poisonous weeds and opiate drugs to seal

The sense in slumber : this is named the bower

Of Unbelief; the other decked, profuse

Of various flowers, told of pleasure wide,—

Of universal bliss,—a mockery

Of all around it and its votaries joy;

This did Unwise with frowning brow disdain,

And to the far-off East uplift his eyes,

But dull and heavy clouds rolled thick between

The once warm brilliance of those realms and him,

And downward sweeping veiled the glorious cross;

Nor East nor West was sight to cheer his gaze—

A wilful wanderer!—on high the sun

Fierce blazing downward, deep he heaved a sigh,

Then 'neath his feet laid down the Book, and passed,

With resolution dark and lip compressed,

The threshold of that bower, to death so dear,

Called Unbelief—the portals of the tomb;

And there I watched him wearily reclined,

Ere long in sleep fast bound, anon beheld

The fearful gestures of his evil dreams,

And all the proofs of that fell restlessness

Man cannot kill by slumber.   What the frame

Of clay, to bind the giant power within,

Big with immortal knowledge, when it raves

Untiring there ? its tyranny alone,

The mortal being's sure destruction proves.

He slept ! he slept ! and to the West drew on

The wearying day ; nor did he see or fear

The peril that his troubled spirit saw,

And strove with supernatural power to him

Thus to communicate.   " Unhappy one !

When shalt thou wake ?" I cried, " Oh, when arise ?

Ere night comes on ? ere, hurried to the vale,

Its raging torrents loud before thee foam,

And thou, in wild tumultuous tempest lost,

Must onward go ?"   He slept ! yes, still he slept !

   *   *   *   *   *

Sleep has no balm, no downiest pillow is

Soft, for the fevered brow, whose aching throb

Would lose in sleep its madness : when the frame

Reposes, then the spirit does not rest

More than, when dust commingles with its dust,

The soul to ashes turns ; continued life

Have both, or that continual state of woe

Inflicting torment on the body, toil

Interminable ; and what then is that ?

Can it a life be named, albeit it has

Cessation of existence none, which death is called,

Yet void of all that to the name of life

Adds good ? it is that state of life far worse

Than death itself, whose victim may be said,

For ever in the bitterest pangs of death

Chained fast, thus ever dying, NEVER *dead !*

Sleep has no balm for him, to sleep, who flies

From horrors which increase around the while,

To which he soon must wake, and whose first thought

Must, waking, be of them, and earliest sense,

That of their presence and unblest demands.

No crimson streak of morn upon his couch,

Or heated pillow, when Unwise awoke,

Its cooling brightness threw; but haggard, wild,

I saw him rise, come forth, and gaze around ;—

No sparkling river there, no flowers of bloom,

No mossy banks, or heavenly hills afar,

In distance beautiful, he saw; and ah !

No Book of shining page, no shelt'ring cross !

In the black West I saw the sun appear,

Half fall'n beneath the wailing, wide, green sea ;

Still fiercely scowling on the clouds that sought

Too soon to quench him : lower now he sinks,

And dark they brood in counsel for a storm,

With shaggy brows o'erhung, in dark embrace

Of boding whispers chill ; and then no more

I saw the sun ; a sickly light the sky

Gave forth, for suddenly the West had seized

One latent torch, and winged it as a shaft :

Swift from its livid root aloft it sprang,

And, darting devious through the ambient gloom,

Lit all the aërial elements perplexed

With flaming fury, and to Heaven's heart

White 'neath his sable garments rent in twain,

Relentless quivered : then the wounded sky,

Shaken with strong and loud convulsions groaned,

From pole to pole, and on the stricken head

Of him o'ertaken shed its drops of blood,

Heavy and frequent ; he, in fearful flight,

Ran here and there unconscious, and his face

Hid from the revelry of nature wild.

Much dreaded I the valley of the flood

Would soon receive him then ; when through the glare

Of tempest on his path, a roll I saw

Coiled nigh the brink of a capacious pit,

At hand wide-gaping, down whose sides at times

From ledge to ledge fell forks of lightning red,

Each chasm lighting : here he stooped, to see

If that were some stray leaf by whirlwind driven
From his lost guide, and read with pallid fear
Its name Despair, and horrid counsel given,—
Deep in those caverns shelter to procure !
The clouds were cleft ; a gust caught up the roll,
And flung it fiercely in his streaming face,
Damp with the chilly gore of murdered time !
Yet, at that direful moment, did he gain
Strength this to spurn, and as the severed worm,
By its own writhings shrinks from danger's way,
Crawled from the dungeon's opening brink in pain,
Then, powerless stretched, his bitter tones recalled
The rising morn and all, that fair and good,
He foolishly despised, and slept away ;
Then blamed his folly and transgressions all,
And wept aloud. · Now, as he wept, it seemed
That the destroying angel had refrained
To add his voice to that of some blest choir
Whose hallelujah swelled above the storm !

D

Again loud peals of heavy thunder rolled,

Drowning its harmony; but sudden flew

A vivid flash along the East,—lit up

A distant rock, and for an instant there

The Cross displayed ! bright on its grassy height,

Untouched and fair; then all grew dark again.

New life into the frame of him laid low

Appeared to burst :—" Oh, if," he earnest cried—

" If that might yet be gained ! Oh, Thou so bright !

Where now the guide Thou gavest me, or how

Thither to fly, I know not ; all I know

Is misery extreme; here—even here

Once more to me, for mad presumption false

So justly stricken, that best Book reveal ?"

On which I did behold a wondrous light

Come sailing through the far, far skies along;—

A Dove, whose silv'ry wings shed soft around,

Its path of flight, a glow as that which spreads

Through the thin vapour driv'n on starry night

Across the full moon's face, which, from the hills,

A shining track had left ; its flight was stayed

O'erhead, where on the earth the suppliant knelt,—

The sodden earth,— and sweet refulgence cast

Upon his pale cold brow; then, gently down,

Its pinions stooped, attracting, as it flew,

The wand'rer on ; entranced, but trembling still,

He followed, till, alighting suddenly,

Among the pages of his long-lost Book

It fluttered, and each letter bathed in light !

What joy was his ! unto his heart he clasped

The prize, th' unspoken prize ; then did a voice,

On thunder borne, loud bid him " up" and " on !"

From worst destruction ; stumbling oft he flew :—

" Where was his pathway ?" ask you; " had he found

The right, the living way ?" Ah ! that bright Dove

Did trace it with his pinions bright, and lead

Straight on and swiftly : clasping close the Book,

That radiant one he followed, faint but firm ;

His feeble strength had failed to bear him on,

But oh ! that glorious, glowing sight gave power

Beyond conception's might ! and, nearing now

The rising rock, more strong it grew : yet here—

Here too, was danger rife ; one moment then,

Shook the fierce skies with baffled wrath severe,

And shook the earth that yawned for him in vain

His heart beat loud, his trembling hand let go

The Book ; but, hastily to grasp again

The falling treasure, both were wide outspread :

Swift time was short ; *one* leaf alone torn forth,

That grasp retained, *but of the Cross it spake*,

Thus all was well ! upon the Rock he sprang,

The everlasting Rock ! when all things else

Rolled shattered into chaos ; safe from thence

Beheld afar the suffering plains, the streams

Run red to cataracts of woe unknown ;

The gaping pit, for ever crying, " Give,"

Gather creation's broken fragments in,

A flaming waste, and smoky columns hurled

From all its surface to the frowning sky :

Did he then shudder ?   Nay, why does yon tree

Skyward extend its scorched and naked arms ?

Why rocks it so on earth's convulsive breast ?

Does not the giant champion of the storm —

The veteran tempest, cruelly embrace

Those time-seared limbs, and with its mother earth

Drag for the mastery ? the deed is done ;

And from each wounded pore, the bleeding root

Is torn ; then to the tyrant useless more

The whole vast bulk is hurled upon the soil ;

But not a breath that one bright leaf has stirred,

Or shaken from the rose's fragrant bloom,

Which now the penitent delighted plucks,

One drop of early dew ! as round the cross,

On which the shining Dove now rested white,

His arm was flung, and on its golden side,

His brow was pressed, and tears of joy he shed,

High o'er the vale, and beautifying all

With calm, surpassing beauty, I beheld

Clouds like the wings of angels, and a form

Whose fairness robed them all in stainless white,

Smiling on him below; as 'twere to say,

" Some there are here thou knowest ; soon I come ! "

These were the Eastern hills, but not beyond :

A little step, when rested there awhile,

He who was lost and found must higher go.

Now whilst I, thankful for his great escape,

Did bless the love which o'er this one had watched,

Methought his voice, so late in anguish raised,

Or spent in terror's whisper, thus exclaimed :—

" When thou, sweet Dove, at blush of dawn shalt fly ;

When thou shalt upward soar to brighter realms,—

Regions where He who made this path for me

Hath homes prepared for such as weary are

Which Peace, my gentle Peace, has long enjoyed,

Waiting to bid me to its blissful joy

Glad welcome;—when thou there shalt soar, sweet

    Dove,

Together travelling at that sunny hour,

We'll to the hills,—we'll to the heavenly hills."

       *   *   *   *   *

. Filled with the gentlest breathings of delight

Sent up from Eden's green, luxurious fields,

Did airy float a mist of heavenly birth ;

Its essence music, soft and ravishing,

Now faint, now near : within it ceaseless roamed

Bright forms, whose voices of harmonious love

This music was, which as the airs of spring

Spread grateful round, in pairs or groups they passed.

There strayed a family ; a sister here

Beside her brother walked.   Now louder burst

The ethereal strain, and rapture filled my soul !

Light glorious beamed !—it was the morning sun,

The music ceased—I woke, it was a dream !

MISCELLANEOUS POEMS.

THOUGHTS

ON

A NEW-YEAR'S MORNING.

" Lord, thou hast been our dwelling-place in all
generations."—*Ps.* xc. 1.

ARISE, my soul ! the burial shroud of night
Another year conceals,—for ever gone !
Wake to the call of Hope and purpose new,
Wrapt in the rising year, from depths unseen
That beckon on, and nerve for every toil.

First conscious breath that wakes the still pro-
    found
Of thought unstartled, waft to heaven a prayer,
On wings of Faith to Time's Creator borne,—
And thine immortal ! future inhabitant
Of that Eternity His presence fills.

Now swift as dawn, and as his shooting rays
Far multiplied diffuse, do thoughts return
Of things which have been, and shall be no more,
For good or evil fixed or unfulfilled.
Methinks beside an ancient tree I stand;
Wide spread its branches bare, and chill o'erhung,
Where Thames thro' rural meads his stately flood
Rolls on, content to bless these scenes of peace,
Nor court the busier crowded haunts of men.
Here Friendship and Instruction sweet combined
Charms every shade, and sounds in every wave
A second music lovelier than its own,

Part of my being! not forgetful now   .

As once,—too blest,—to shut these eyes on all —

This heart on peace — if gratitude most due

To God and man engrossed not all thy joy.

Here let me rest beneath this wintry shade,

As stealing twilight smooths the ruffled tide ;

Eve should foretell repose, yet no soft rest

Joyous I hail as all things round me do,

From troublous turmoil free, and losing self

With all its wants, in meditative praise,

Still busy Self distracts the general peace :

So stands amid the forest's quivering pines,

In richest green arrayed, the lifeless tree,

Blest in no season, as they slow revolve,

With garment vernal; and whilst far and near,—

As thro' their midst aërial breathings creep,—

Each other bough its every leaf employs

To swell the gentle harmony of all,

His creaking branches ceaselessly repine,

And spread their melancholy woes abroad.

Swift time rolls on, and welcome changes come,

Of place and scene, yet never strange or new,

Since there the truant eye, with reason fond,

Of watchful mem'ry dwelt when morn and eve,

With light and shadow marked the gliding days.

Oh Hills endear'd ! Ye vales of Cambria, hail !

'Twere hard without applause to gaze on thee,

Trembling to meet the earliest glance of spring,

His tenderest voice, and with a blush be won !

There silv'ry Usk, by many a dear retreat

Of humming shade, reluctant holds his way;

Or listens charmed, in some grove-darkened dell,

To lone Seclusion's sigh, where willows weep;

Oh, favoured stream ! the music of thy flow

Is soft as recollection born of thee;

As varied all — as full of ling'ring love

Low whispering to the woods its fairy tale;

For oft thy murmurs melancholy fall,

When through the deepening twilight, plaintive
    sounds
The ringdove's coo from out his hushed retreat,
Or night surrounds the neighb'ring hills with gloom.
Hand of the Past! now lead me soft again,
Where once I sat at moonlit hour alone ;—
The place of many graves : few deem when there
Of higher worth the pleasures of an hour,
Than Duty's glorious, best, divine reward !
A solemn sight ! scarce half one straggling ray
Can gild the cold dark side of any grave,
So close they throng ! but on th' engraven stone,
Falls broad and pale, to teach the grief of some,
The hope of others, and the end of all :
Nay—not the end on earthly mould inscribed,
Or written there or read,—its type alone ;
He who of old on Patmos' isle was cast,
Saw where 'twas writ, and heard its wonders read
By Majesty Most High, as shall be done,

Whilst Heaven and Earth and Hell, with all they hold,

Silent attend thro' all the vast of space.

Now spread the sails—my native land, adieu!

What infant song, what feeble accents thee

Shall speak beloved, and wing the thoughts they
      would?

Faint falls the light on Albion's mist-clad cliffs,

Where, far and faint along the winding strand,

Low-glimmering lights soft smile a sweet farewell,—

And all around is revelry and sea!—

How blest is he who, being born to die,

Is "born again" to live when death is past,

Immortal conqueror of mortal ills!

His the possession of unshaken peace,

Seal of its truth, and Life's eternal spring;

His the kind solace of a Father's care

From parent far, an elder brother's aid

And counsel wise, when, wandering long, he dreams

Of Home forsaken, or at times recalls

A brother's voice, or sister's sunny smile;

And more the living comforts of his soul,

His sense of being and enduring changed,

Bright treasures incorruptible above,

Sure as the throne of Heaven; for oft when there

His hands he lifts and "Abba, Father," cries,

Through all creation seems a voice to say,

" Son, ever with me, *all* I have is thine !"

But twilight gathers now, and near the vale

Of Death's cold shade, where all his trust's assailed,

Struck with the bolts of Hell, but not dismayed

In utter ruin or tumultuous flight:

Still on the Christian goes, the "rod and staff"

Him solace there, his Saviour's arm sustains!

Perchance some steadfast pilgrim, strong in faith,

Deems e'en the taste of Jordan's water sweet,

As soft its music lulls him to repose !

The flood rolls by : upon the blissful brink,

Bereft of sin, bereft of self, he stands :

E

On either side one shining seraph waits;

Each, silent, meditates on Love divine,

Or courts his first acclaims of pure delight,

With hints celestial or with harps of love.

Now to the gates of pearl upborne they rise,

And raptures inconceivable within,

On Zion's hill and round the throne prepared:—

Such was sweet matter of rejoicing thought

At noon or silent eve, or when the lull

Of heavy night mute listened to the waves

Roll dirge-like round, and melancholy moan

" Deep unto deep; " then oftentimes would come

One who would whisper " It is I ! "—'twas He

At midnight on the darksome billows walked

Of Galilee's rough tide; blest messenger

Of peace as then, whom " winds and seas obey : "

Perchance at intervals a sound would rise

Of hearty praise unburdened, or of prayer,

Anxious as that, on Peniel's plain, which craved

At dawn a benediction,—Israel's plea.

Adieu, ye days of endless life the spring!

Long shall I think of thee, both when I roam

Far in the strangers' land, or home I love;

Why not when in that blest abiding Home

"Not made with hands, eternal in the sky?"

SYMPATHY.

AN ODE.

CLEAR Harp, whose nightly murmurs spread
  Melodious through the sacred shade,
Where pensive Sorrow oft has shed
  Fast tears, to none beside betrayed ;
If Nature knows thy soothing call,
  And answers to th' Eolian sweep,—
Why not those strains as sweetly fall
On mortal bosom, and bid all
  Its warm affections weep ?

Oh gifts of Earth, from chaos rude
    Uplifted by th' Eternal's hand!—
Oh Earth, of chaos formed, how good —
    How great—how beautiful ye stand!
How each on each serenely smile!
    How tune the universal song,
That peals thro' Nature's temple aisle
One-voiced, till on her funeral pile
    Falls voiceless every tongue!

Oh thou, for whom their fairest all
    Smiles sweetest, wakes the heavenliest lay,
How dark the treachery of that fall
    Which made thee cease to love as they!
His due Hosannas cease to raise,
    High seated on the Eternal throne
Of unreached glory, and, with praise,
To share, thro' all thine earthly days,
    His spotless gifts, as one.

Inspire my lay, O soul of Love!
   From fallen man to brother given :
Essence of Him who sways above
   The sceptre of adoring Heaven !
Once pure thro' all this world of old,
   When far Euphrates' banks, and rare
Havilah, round whose soil of gold
Encircling Pison proudly rolled,
   Stretched under Eden fair ;—

And stainless 'neath th' approving smile
   Which sealed the word that spake them good ;
Ere harboured they the serpent's wile,
   Or brother spilt a brother's blood.—
Hence, theme unblest !—thee, valleys sweet —
   Rocks, rising hills and buzzing groves,
I sing, by sin's still doubting feet
Unbrushed, unstartled by the greet
   Of any voice but Love's.

On Earth's fair face no fallen tree

    Has torn the forest's turfy floor;

No shipwreck o'er the spacious sea

    Is scattered to the sounding shore.

Ah! beauteous form,—whate'er thou be,—

    Glad animate with heavenly breath

Thro' all thy radiant frame, to thee

Death's but a name—thou ne'er didst see

    The pale, cold form of Death!

Thou hast not felt the rankling dart

    That cleft in twain the cord it left;

That empty hollowness of heart

    Of all it loved, by time bereft,

But, vocal with the general Spring,

    Dost lift the obedient anthem high

At Phœbus' earliest sign, nor fling

The lyre away, when twilight's wing

    Is waved across the sky.

Responsive harp, be joy thy theme,

   O'er-pass the ages of the past,

And all that gloomy troubled dream

   From which a world is waked at last.

From Life to Life, o'er Death's loud flood,

   A bridge suspend;—from Eden high

Where Eve, ere yet the fatal food

She tasted, Hope's fair emblem stood,

   To night-veil'd Calvary.

There may the weeping wonderer hear

   Of blissful Paradise regained;

First Eden's sentence dark and drear

   Made portal to a better land.

" Remember me, my dying Lord,"

   Is all the suff'ring sinner's prayer,

" When to thy kingdom fair restored ;"—

" To-day"—Immanuel's gladdening word—

   " Shalt thou be with me there !"

Hail, voices blest of Him who gave
    Example holiest, purest, best;
Low murmuring o'er a kinsman's grave,
    To give some aching spirit rest;
There breathes thy spell as that whose strain
    First sought the hills of Salem nigh,
" Thy brother"—friend—" shall rise again ;"
It soothes of every heart the pain
    As hers of Bethany.

He too has wept;—for whom ?—Behold,
    Sad eye by sore affliction proved,
(Not all as did the Jews of old,)
    The lonely weepers how He loved !
He loved thy lost one, and hath led
    His soul where flowers unfading grow ;
He loves the mourners, and hath said
How precious are the tears they shed,
    By His own sacred woe.

'Tis love unselfish that must bind
    The bleeding wound, and soothe its pain,
And the same bond, in grief entwined
    Can make two hearts no longer twain;
Oh, who can tell with careless voice
    What the first thrill of pleasure deep,
Approving his determined choice
" To joy with them that do rejoice,
    And weep with them that weep !"

They *will* be rich who now are poor,
    And those be comforted who mourn;
As Lazarus to the rich man's door,
    To beg the uneaten morsels, borne.
And if no other cause compel,
    'Twere well their woes on earth to share,
With them in equal bliss to dwell
In heaven's courts, nor see from hell
    Their envied pleasures there.

In fair prosperity of heart
   Be't ours to soothe ungentle care;
Those blessings which the blest impart
   Their tasted virtues with them bear.
Oft as a sigh from desert drear,
   When like distresses lurk within,
That voice, which meant to soothe and cheer,
Low falters with a trickling tear
   Of things which might have been ; —

And shall the bubble, lifted high
   Where mountain billows awful form,
Ask wherefore ocean swells ? or why
   The rending heavens are racked with storm ?
Or ocean's self less mighty, found
   Upon the universal sea
Of ordered things, whose only bound
The Wisdom that enclasps them round,
   Ask, why should these things be ?

This from all finite knowledge shields
 Too great conceptions for the soul,
As through all time those icy fields
 That gather lasting round the pole;
Once entered there, canst thou retain
 An only life, to breathe alone?
And shall thy mental vision vain
E'er overreach, one step to gain
 In that untraversed zone?

Thus joy should still untiring seek
 For sorrow, half its gifts to share;
The fickle dealings of a week
 May cloud its smiles with cruel care.
Be't that the mourner never rise
 To kiss the hand that eased his pain;
The smile that lights his closing eyes
Shall be a sevenfold costlier prize
 Than all the worldling's gain!

  *   *   *   *   *

Borne back through vanished ages long,
　Around my path like spectres rise
The states and battlements of song,
　Their orators and warriors wise.
Pale Luna's beams at distance fall
　O'er many a vestige, dimly cast,
Of crumbling column, giant wall,
That speaks in hollow accents all
　The Carthage of the past.

These all are lost, his form to see
　Who sits a stony figure there;
Content in solitude to be
　Where it were second life to share;—
To share disgrace that both might gain
　New glory, could her fallen throne
Stir all his heart to feel a pain
For others' sorrows prostrate lain,
　Not wholly for his own.

There might the exiled Roman find
    The memory of departed days
Fall lightly on the monarch mind,
    That rules the ruin it surveys.
There from its tombs and ashes great,
    Beneath the solemn midnight moon,
A prouder Carthage might create,
And, leaving thought of former state,
    With Hannibal commune!

But ruined Self compelled thee lone,—
    Ambition's and thy rival's toy,—
Where every spectacle makes known
    How man may man's best work destroy,
Yea, ruined Self; now see thee led
    In fiercer power to Rome again:
Hear, hear the wailing o'er the dead;
The streets with human gore are red,
    The houses filled with slain.

'Tis thus th' unhumbled despot feels
   His people's wants — his country's need ;
And thus in costly sheath conceals
   The sword that makes that country bleed.
Such deeds are his whose heart had been
   Best pleased its like distress to find ;—
A towerless base whereon to lean,—
Where every trace was fittest seen
   Some ruin of the mind.

More noble he who, deeming woe
   Hung o'er Athenia's spotless fame,
Brought counsel to his bitterest foe,—
   Death daring ; well "the Just" his name :
And Salamis, with his, thy name,
   Unmixed with guile, through time shall be
The secret traitor's open shame,
The record of sublimest fame,
   The spell of Sympathy.

Love — love thy friend; but also " love
    Thine enemy,"—Divine command!
Where'er thou dwellest or dost rove;
    Thy neighbour, or thy native land,
So their prosperity shall thrill
    Untasted pleasures thro' thy soul;
And still unaltering — loving still —
Ye'll have at length one joy, one will,
    And share one glorious whole!

Oh pardon, Thou! whose heavenly tone
    Doth teach me, while I weary roam
Beneath, I cannot pass alone
    Along the waves that waft me home:
Still pardon that which is not Thine,
    And perfect that which is begun;
Let Thy blest will alone be mine,
And all I do — intend — design —
    Be to Thy glory done!

The things of Time and Sense appear
  In truest light, severe or kind;
That nothing earthly steal the care
  Intended for the immortal mind.
Nor folly, I had counted wise,
  For Earth, if all its gifts it gave,
Ere barter Life; Time's goodliest prize
Must soon rest, hidden from these eyes,
  Above the covered grave.

To Thy great name my thankful voice
  It loudest anthems still shall raise;
Nor lonely sorrow, or rejoice,
  Nor lonely pray, nor lonely praise.
And Thou, who knowest all the ways
  Of those whose hearts are sorely riven,
Teach them all earthly bliss decays,
And be thro' everlasting days
  Their bright and tearless heaven!

F

A REVERIE.

THEY loved — but sorrow clouded o'er
    The early sunshine of their love ;
And altered hopes, and trouble sore,
    Shattered what Time could ne'er remove ;

They changed the bright endearing smile,
    Which he, who oft had seen it, deemed
That strange and fascinating wile
    Which shaped his fancies while he dreamed.

Tears followed smiles (how oft they do,—
    All know it ; none pronounce it strange ;
Yet, knowing it, alas how few
    Rejoice, anticipating change !)

Reality is stern when past,
  And robbed of all that made it fair ;
A frowning outline, cold and vast—
  An empty void alone is there.

They loved,—the tears they often shed
  Were tears of joy, yet still *were* tears ;
And as they fell it seemed they said,—
  " Earth's joys are only joyous fears."

Strange sorrow - joy—to hope and feel
  A something bright may be in store,
Which months and even days may steal,
  And leave all gloomier than before.

They loved,—but tempests rose and chased
  The beams from love's affrighted sky ;
Yet earth alone these storms defaced—
  It all grew bright, at last, on high.

They saw the fields, which late outspread
  So beauteous, desolate and bare;
They wept above the rose's bed,
  For half-blown buds hung blighted there.

They saw the home,—Ah! all to tell
  Were sad as that forgotten scene,
Or echoes of the last farewell,
  With broken voice, and sobs between,—

" 'Twas only earth those storms defaced,
  It all at last grew bright on high,"
And from the dark and dismal waste
  Upturned to heaven the tearful eye.

They loved;—forget the sad, sad tale
  Which clouded o'er their early love:
O'er blighted prospects draw the veil
  'Twixt thee and heaven, and look above.

There is a land — a fair, fair land—

   From change and sorrow far removed,

Where still they wander hand in hand,

   And angels whisper still " they loved!"

THE YEW-TREE'S SHADE.

" Beneath those rugged elms, that Yew-tree's shade."
GRAY'S *Elegy*.

IN MEMORIAM.

DOMAINS of Silence ! here, in deep repose,

Lie hushed the ills, th' inconstancies of Time ;

Nor strife, to strew the daily path with woes,

Can haunt the footsteps as they heav'nward climb :

Here has Bereavement long-enduring knelt,

Returned to see the roses bloom and fade,

Here watched the winter's dreary mantle melt,

And grass grow green, beneath the Yew-tree's shade.

Chill o'er the turf hangs many a drooping bough,

With kindly care, its soft and solemn cloud;

As many mourners darken Death's cold brow,

And shield the pallid bareness of his shroud,—

A dark-green canopy,—and far beneath

Floats on the music of a light cascade,

No more to rapture with melodious breath

Their hearts who slumber 'neath the Yew-tree's
     shade :

Nor ever may the song terrestrial move,

Or gaudy glitter of a world of show,

Where sound the ecstasies of heavenly love,

Where crystal floods thro' fields celestial flow.

No sad complaint may pass the gate of peace,

Where, loosed at length, life's heavy load is laid :

Thus far they come,—and here for ever cease,—

All pain and labour, 'neath the Yew-tree's shade.

There is a tomb where waves the wild flower free,
And fragrant blooms, beside a marble stone,
Upreared where one wide-spreading, ancient tree,
Sighs over Youth's cold sepulchre alone,
No stranger bough disturbs its pensive form,
Where oft his more than youthful fancy strayed ;
Its vigil shields that fair tomb from the storm,
And guards the slumberer with a Yew-tree's shade.

Dear friend, how silent, sacred, is the scene ! —
Thy grassy bed, beneath that chosen tree
Whose branches ever-grieving, ever-green,
Wave o'er thy resting-place, and weep for thee.
Yet better there to bend o'er Friendship's bier,
Than midst the world, for love sincere betrayed,
To drop unrecognised a bitter tear,
Too sad and earthly for this holy shade.

A HISTORICAL PICTURE ON THE BANKS OF THE WYE.

"Vocal no more, since Cambria's fatal day,
  To high-born Hoel's harp, or soft Llewellyn's lay."
                                    GRAY's *Bard*.

OLD Piercefield now looks proudly down, the deep-
  rolled waters o'er

Where winding Wye shall glide along through
  Slaughter's vale no more:

From crag to crag no warrior shout awake her cliff-
  girt side,

Rise on the roar of wint'ry storm, or summer's
  peace deride:

Dull kite, upborne above the wood on slow convulse-
  less wing,

Nor kestrel startles in his cave, to hear the weapons
  ring;

But oft at eve, in hollow wail of solitary woe,

The night-owl hoots his dark applause at day's
    departed glow.

Here doth the conscious river, nigh unto its future
    home,

Forget swift Youth's more sparkling course, content
    sedate to roam,

Much as the thought-directed flow of life's maturer
    day,

When deep Eternity appears not very far away.

Primæval grandeur, purpled wood, and giddy step-
    less height,

Of shelving rock stoop shadowy o'er with ancient
    moss bedight,

But well I ween that mansion grey, the monarch of
    the glen,

Sees all effaced the transcript fell of red ambition's
    pen.

Ye days of Cambrian chivalry! your nursery was
   song,
It flowed commixed with princely blood the burning
   veins along,
Each pulse-throb flung the rapture forth from some
   deep-hidden string,
Each heart-beat taught some chieftain-bard of former
   fame to sing!
Ye days of Cambrian chivalry! that lyre had better
   been
Beneath the flow of angry Wye than on its banks of
   green,
Whose last wild note a bitter wail adown the current
   flung—
A slave's the hand which tore its chords, and chains
   the theme they sung.

The chieftain is to battle gone, the lady to her bower,
To sigh and weep in solitude at twilight's stilly hour;

From ether blue the stars look bright upon this
world below,

As all like them should sighless be, and ever smiling
glow.

In Rhuddlan's battlemented walls does England's
monarch stay,

Exulting in his brighter hopes till dawn of early day;

Exulting to have learnt at length Llewellyn and his
train

Their mountain-fastnesses have left to meet him on
the plain.

There is a murmur, as the sea heaves off its troubled
breast,

When muttering gales begin to lift the billow from
its rest;

To gather in its masses slow, embodied soon to rise,

A pillared waterspout of death into the howling
skies :

There is a murmur hurried on throughout the Briton
    ranks,

A wrathful, anguish-stricken groan on Wye's tumul-
    tuous banks;

And many a lip, to pain compressed, drives on the
    joyless sound,—

Llewellyn lies, and long shall lie, upon the stainèd
    ground!

Urge! Mortimer, the day is thine! What! dar'st
    not know it yet?

In truth not easily thy fears old Snowdon's broils
    forget!

But Nature here refuses more her barriers to allow,

To splinter back the steel-bound darts thy skilful
    archers throw.

Llewellyn! there is death, alas, this day to more than
    thee,

And they who live but long to die, they live not to
    be free!

Say, heard'st thou, with a duller ear than was thy
 wont of yore,
What wail arose to know that thou hadst fall'n to
 rise no more ?

Say, didst thou, half in slumber see, that flash of steel
 on high,
As lifts the bleeding eagle's wing ere vigourless it lie ?
The Saxon mass as on they rushed, like giant's tot-
 tering frame,
Hurled back ; for blighting was the scorch of Hope's
 expiring flame ;
Then didst thou to repose recline ere yet a glimmering fell
Upon that sudden torch, a tale of coming gloom to
 tell ;
Nor learn at length the bitter truth,— thine ancient
 line was o'er,
As lord of Cambria's beauteous hills, and vales, and
 rivers more ?

The sun is red on Severn's wave, far blushing to
    his beam,

And red with an unearthlike red on Wye's blood-
    weeping stream !

Grey Cader Idris far away has caught the spreading
    wail,

And dark Plinlimmon's torrents sob to night's im-
    passioned gale !

And there are gatherings, chill, forlorn, on Arvon's
    sea-damp sand,

Of those whose strength no more can prop their
    falling fatherland ;

For few are they, and most are scarr'd, their faces
    deadly white,

Look terrible through moonlight pale, a spectral
    scene of night.

Behold, the seers' white streaming locks wild strew
    the solemn air,

For hoary sage and minstrel hold their last assembly
    there ;

No sounding harpstring's echo falls, a hero's deeds
    to tell

To all the listening rocks around, as formerly it
    fell.

There is a gentle, lonely sigh, in moonlit myrtle
    bower,

A dimness crossing beauty's eye at twilight's stilly
    hour ;

But no endearing tale is near to change that weary
    sigh,

No winding horn upon the hills to brighten up that
    eye ! —

Now rests no stained, no war-torn sod, on Wye's
    soft banks of green ;

For years have passed, and stol'n the trace of that
    which once has been :

The merle's sweet madrigal is heard at morning's
    earliest hour;

There springs the white anemone, the woodland's
    cherished flower:

Nor ever is there discord dark amid the mountain's
    rife —

When brother meets with brother there, there are no
    words of strife;

No memory of those distant days, that bitter blood-
    stained feud,

Their fathers knew, less blest than they, in darker
    ages rude.

Sweet Severn, of Plinlimmon birth, her native land
    to bless,

First tastes the pleasures of that land, her Cambria's
    kind caress;

Then bears the beauties of those hills along a flowery
    bed,

G

Where lovely Albion's valleys bright are by their
    virtues fed :

Thus ever with her sister stream, the rich romantic
    Wye,

May winter's storms their bosoms fan as summer
    evening sigh ;

Still peace adorn the gentle banks their shining
    waters lave,

Harmonious resting on the brink, harmonious in the
    cave.

TO BRECON.

WRITTEN AT SEA.

SWEET vale! no voice of Ocean e'er
   Thy still retirement knew;
No sea-storm lurks in sullen lair
   Amid thy mountains blue;—
Loved Brecon, absent from the gaze
   That billows bound for me,
How oft the flight of memory strays
   Instinctive back to thee!

Borne swift across the briny waste,
　　Back to some sheltering wood,
Where, winding green, thy vale is traced
　　By Usk's transparent flood,—
Bright Usk ! the woodland shade at eve,
　　When sunset rays divide,
Smiles, as their latest beam they leave
　　Upon thy golden tide.

There yet will ling'ring wishful rest
　　One Time-existing ray,
Waiting to die upon thy breast,
　　When life's full beams decay :
Thus, hastening on, sometimes a flower
　　Beside our path we find,
Which leaves not at its fading hour
　　But beauty's blight behind.

A SISTER'S VOICE.

" But thy soft murmuring
Sounds sweet, as if a sister's voice reproved."
                              BYRON.

How often on my heedless ear,

In days gone by, that gentle tone

Had fallen soft; but ah! though near

The words were breathed, I did but hear,—

  Not half they meant was known!

Now, stealing o'er the moonlit wave

With the wild music of the sea,

Lost words from many an early grave,

Words which a gentle sister gave,

  Come sadly back to me.

I close mine eyelids, and I stand
Where no deep billows roll around,
For in my childhood's far-off land
I seem to clasp her soft white hand,
　　And listen to the sound.

I weep not when they rest again
Upon the wide unvaried sea,
Or sigh, remembering how vain
The music of the murmuring main
　　'Twixt that loved land and me.

For Heaven's calm light upon the deep,
So oft by cruel tempests driven,
Forbids me, while those tempests sleep,
And starry worlds shine bright, to weep ;—
　　And thou didst speak of Heaven.

May angels, loved one, softly say,

Whilst thou art sleeping, " Do not fear—

Thy brother, though he's far away,

Still loves, while billows round him play,

His sister's voice to hear."

THE CASCADE.

UNDER the darkening bridge it ran,
Into the sunshine swift and bright,
And there its fairy sport began,
Leaping from off the giddy height :
Young primroses, to see the sight,
Looked up in pretty groups and smiled ;
And the wild woodland's fav'rite child,
   The delicate anemone,
   Its perilous descent to see
Grew pale, and trembled with affright.

It sparkled in the May-morn sun,
Shooting its silver arrows round;
Rested, and then more wildly run,
Enraptured by its own sweet sound:
O'er many a devious ledge it wound
Its moss-paved path, and crooked fall,
Admired and wondered at by all:
No overshadowing turf, to gain
A lightening kiss, hung o'er in vain
    Betwixt the bridge and level ground.

One instant—*but* one instant—there,
With mute and glowing smile it stood,—
Trembled at what itself could dare,
And wandered on in thoughtful mood,
Down-winding through the solemn wood:
On either velvet side was spread
A varied carpet, and its bed

Smooth pebbles formed ; in this retreat
Soft sounds of Naiads' tiny feet
   Oft fall, or wood-nymphs whispers brood.

And here sometimes, when all around,
And in the lofty boughs, is still,
Nor near or far is heard a sound
Except the tinkling of the rill,
A breath from summer skies will fill
The clustering leaves, and gently shake
The flow'rets sleeping in the brake,
Then murmur while the mavis sings,
And all the wakened valley rings,
   Strange tales, which all their bosoms thrill.

There came a stranger to these halls,
In beautiful disguise, when bright
The May-sun sparkled on the falls,
And all things wondered at the sight ;

They said that morning, that the light
Looked through the branches wond'rous fair,—
They laughed, but nothing else was there :
She came all beautiful,— and still
Her voice is in the sparkling rill,
   Sweet, heavenly music, day and night.

May 4, 1860.

THE POETRY OF PEACE.

" Mercy and truth are met together ; righteousness and peace
have kissed each other."—*Ps.* lxxxv. 10.

A CONSCIENCE basking in the smile of Heaven,

Whose noonday sun is holiness and love,

Glad in the consciousness of sins forgiven

And justice satisfied, can rise above

Earth's trifles and earth's cares, and cast below

A look of peace ineffable : but so

Is that clear conscience made of Christ's pure mind

A blest partaker, that ere long the woe,

Darkening a world to its own interests blind,

Shrouds the bright spirit's radiance, and with Him

Who over Salem wept, the eye of peace grows dim.

Immortal being ! who are they all fair,

The limit of whose sight is perfect bliss ? —

They've reached the heavenly world, and, happy there,

Have ceased to weep for misery in this ;

Not one inhabitant their eyes behold

Without a robe of white, or crown of gold.

This, then, is peace ineffable, but far

Beyond the earthly, as those things untold

Which fancy paints beyond experience are

In real life ; but how can thought increase

Or fancy paint the bounds of perfect, lasting peace ?

LINES WRITTEN IN AN ALBUM.

Not to the sandy beach, where yesterday
You walked and talked, do you return to find
The footprints of a friend now far away,—
Waves have rolled there and left no trace behind :
Not in the hollow moanings of the wind
Come back the voices which afar it bore ;
Another pathway is to thee assigned,
Thine inmost heart's recesses to explore,
There to behold his form, and hear his voice once
    more.

There something heard and treasured quick recalls
The tone in which 'twas uttered, and again,
Fresh on the fancy as at first, it falls,
Bringing its first amount of joy or pain;
No accent there an entrance sought in vain,
Or like a solitary echo came,
Which for an instant only can remain;
For there, distinct to mem'ry as his name,
He stands whose words they were, as when he spake
    —the same.

This is the book where they who come and go
Leave here and there a trace, and nothing more,
Not soon effaced by Time's impetuous flow,
As faint impressions on the sandy shore;
And here the forms which you have seen before
Of absent friends, or friends long passed away,
Some hasty line first faintly will restore,
    And then the thought more perfectly pourtray,
Showing you how they passed their little earthly day.

Then you, who may these varied pages turn,

Let not dull thoughtlessness make vain your toil,

Or rude contempt, your nobler wish to learn

The simplest truths, with tone sarcastic spoil :

For loveliest flowers bedeck the lowliest soil,

And depths of forest unexplored perfume,

Far from the busy world's perpetual broil,

Making a Paradise of earthly gloom,

And beautifying e'en the precincts of the tomb.

1860.

THE MIRAGE.

A Fragment.

Far o'er Sahara's waste the pilgrim's eye
Measures his labour's dread futurity;
But far or near, to soothe his anguish keen,
No palmy foliage specks the hazy scene,—
When all at once his filmy eyes behold
A lucid lake across th' horizon rolled.
"Sweet hope!" he cries; "begone, despairing
      thought!
How kind the toil this matchless hour that brought!
There, from the basin of some crystal pool,
These parching lips shall sip the liquid cool;
My sandals loosed, these wayworn feet shall lave
Their burning wounds beneath the glassy wave.

H

Ye'll soon be there, my trembling steps," he cries;
" Yet, oh ! how distance mocks these aching eyes !
How want deceives !   What giddy languor dim
Sickens my soul, and makes my senses swim."

    Borne onward still by false excitement wild,
Reels on his tortured way the desert child;
With gaze transfixed, that swims but wavers not,
Turned on his all of hope — that watery spot :—
Unequal combat ! but at length content —
Its cruel rage to taunt his misery spent —
The misty lake, unwilling yet to stay
Its fearful work accomplished, fades away;
His childhood's dread, the false mirage he knows,
Thinks on the unreached shrine, forgets his woes,—
In one long-holden, unattended breath
Pours forth his soul, and shuts his eyes in death !

        *   *   *   *

THE STORMY PETREL.

.

THE tempest blast, careering wild,
  Whirls high the scattered spray;
Yet mark yon Ocean's storm-nursed child
  Above the billow play :—
So sports o'er Time's tempestuous sea,
  When torn by winds of care,
Some young affection fond and free
  That has been nurtured there.

THE SECRET OF CONTENT.

.

THERE are in this our earthly sphere
Some lowly paths to wisdom dear,
Whose tuneful shades and arbours rare
For more unpleasing scenes prepare,
Which hush the ruder passion's strife
Ere heightened by the ills of life,
And bid the heart its love extend
To those whose steps may never tend
On toil's rough road, to peace or joy,
Or rest, so absent from alloy.
And there is many a lowly cot
Where envy's voice has sounded not,

Or fierce ambition's brand severe

Lit all most sacred and most dear;

To raise before a selfish world

A flame, whose last mad column, hurled

High as the rapid meteor's flame,

Sinks into nothingness or shame,

The ember-smoke of earthly fame.

How dear is such a cottage home!

There never hard misfortunes come,

Save such as chasten hopes too wild

For Nature's loved but humble child;

And teach th' untutored rustic's mind

How sorrow's self to him is kind.

In some secluded hamlet, seen

Deep in the woodland valley green,

The early, wayward flower to tend,

The sprig new sprouting timely bend;

To fit the growing mind to bear

Harsh storms of trouble and of care;

To point the pathway where the view
Slow climbs some mountain prospect blue,
And dark ravines of danger thread
The pass all mortal footsteps tread,—
Oh, this is heaven-approved employ,
The seed of an immortal joy !
Thy locks, thou honoured master, may
Say, " we have grown too early grey,"
And speak of spring delights which fled
Like wintry shadows o'er thine head ;
Perchance those solemn lips may move
A sentence to departed love ; —
'Tis but the vanity of thought
By thee so oft, so truly taught ;
Still faithfully thy part fulfil,
With constant, unrepining will ;
The crown that all thy labour ends
For all will make a just amends :
Perchance when feebleness and age

That vision dims, those floods assuage

Which often told, when brimming o'er,

The tales that others share no more,

The filling eye, the husky tone

Which spake of sorrows not thine own,

And Time's rude hand has snatched from the.

The lightning dart of mirthful glee;

Then shalt thou smile for joy to hear

How some fair boy to mem'ry dear,

The subject of thy watchful toil,

Reared in this undistinguished soil,

Has lived to yield his cultured mind

A store of blessings to mankind.

He too shall to an end attain

Surpassing all of earthly gain,

Who, lost amid the busy throng

That moves life's crowded course along,

Lost to the loving eyes whose care

Must cease to watch his footsteps there,

And filled with all affection's fears

Return to solitude and tears ; —

Yes, he is blest, who thus resigned,

Deems it his chief concern to bind

Around his heart those bonds of truth

That guided all his earliest youth ;

Resolved to cherish and defend

Each sacred relic to the end :

For these shall lead to genuine peace,

Increasing with the mind's increase,

When urged amid the boisterous crowd

To deeds they never had allowed,

He hears, above the unhallow'd din

That rises from the ranks of sin,

Celestial music softly roll

Its rapture o'er his wavering soul ;

Bid all his latent powers arise,

To hail assistance from the skies,

Which gives him perfect victory

O'er all the hosts of infamy.

Oh ! if on life's dim, chequered way,

Where truth is sober, falsehood gay,

'Tis wisdom eager to pursue

Perfection of all beauty true,

More glorious aim unbinds the soul

From fascination's cursed control ;

Leads up to Pisgah's topmost height

And points to Canaan's fields of light ;

Bids him despise the flowery ease

On pleasure's painted couch he sees,

Disdainful driv'n to court the pain,

Which fools, and none but fools, disdain ;

Conducts him at the hour of rest,

In midnight's rustling mantle dressed,

With gentle voice and noiseless tread,

To his accustomed grassy bed,

On cold damp stones to lay his head :

For there the vision he'll behold

In which his life-long tale is told,

From earth into the opening skies

All bright the angel staircase rise,

Its summit the Eternal's throne,

Each midway resting-place his own :

And there, when morning's misty beam

Disperses all the heavenly dream,

His faith of that stone pillow raise

An altar to Jehovah's praise—

Praise for so bright a picture given

Of his own shining path to heaven.

"THE DAYS THAT ARE GONE."

" That bower and its music I never forget ;
　But oft when alone, in the bloom of the year,
　I think is the nightingale singing there yet :
　　Are the roses still bright by the calm Bendemeer ? "
　　　　　　　　　　　　　Lalla Rookh.

WHERE is that spot where at daylight's decline
　The shadows of memory lightly shall fall ;
Like the star of the evening unsullied to shine
　Through life's multiplied visions the brightest of
　　all ?
Who'll seek it where sadness and changes, a cloud,
　O'er the earliest sunbeams of pleasure have drawn ;
Or deem that another so fair is allowed
　As the first of the many bright days that are gone ?

Home of my heart! if thy rocks and thy streams,
   Thy mountains and valleys, mine ever could be,
I had fancied, to sweeten the rest of my dreams,
   That all earth was a garden of roses like thee;
As the cloud that is gilded when passing the moon,—
   There only those tints can its vapours adorn,
For it floats into darkness and vanishes soon,—
   Is life's first golden vapour the days that are gone:

Yet still whilst the sunshine of summer is strong,
   And the arbours of spring-tide are flowerless and
      few,
I'll think on the groves that are bursting with song,
   And the buds of the valley all dripping with dew,
And lost in th' Elysium of shade that they bring,
   Fly back to the beauties and blossoms of morn;
While the air that is burning around me shall ring
   With the voice of my song to the days that are gone.

A REQUEST.

Whenever Prayer directs your eyes
Where parted spirits meet — above,
Seek far away beyond the skies
  For him you love.

There is a hope when absence whelms
These bosoms that too oft despond;
It pierces yonder azure realms,
  And looks beyond:

For not in vain — to end unseen —
The race of being bears us on; —
The beaten course has trodden been
  In ages gone.

Well Folly might the steps attend
Of him who speeds to goal unknown ;
Who feels not if he reach the end
    He'll gain a crown.

Onward we press from Death to Birth
Of lasting Life ; a span is given
For strife ; the starting point is earth,
    The goal is heaven !

The breast may ache in contest swift,
The heart may palpitate for rest : —
On ! seize the prize ! not throbs its gift,
    Or aching breast.

The journey is but short at last,
Then pain will nothing grievous seem,
Or as review'd, when sleep is past,
    A troubled dream : —

Oh! then, when Prayer directs your eyes

Where parted spirits meet—above,

Seek far away beyond the skies

For him you love!

A PROMISE.

As oft toward the heavenly hill
Each fond desire, on wings of air,
Ascends, thy name shall waken still
    The sweetest music there!

Fair as the shades, that even sends,
Flush crimson o'er the sunset sea,
Each cloud of sorrow soft that blends
    With sunny thoughts of thee:

The light of Hope which stedfast burns,
Beyond, is as that Arctic ray
Which, ere its glory's set, returns
    And changes night to day.

Oceans may separate, and years
As drear and stormy sever wide,—
Sorrows, and joys, and hopes, and fears,
  Like shadows through them glide :

But, through the loudest tempest borne,
Shall Memory's whisper, sweet and mild,
Come o'er the gloomy waste forlorn
  Of thousand billows wild :

Till years have hushed to calm repose
This longing heart's uncertain strife,
And sorrow scarce a shadow throws
  Upon the sea of life ;

Then patient trust, refined by days
Of lonely watchfulness and care,
Shall welcome with a song of praise
  The answer to its prayer.

I

" REQUIESCAT IN PACE."

Lines written on visiting the Grave of Sir H. Havelock, at the Alum Bagh near Lucknow.

No monument erected fair,

To honour'd memory, the last

    Regret can rear ;

And all true worth is doomed to share

Too oft, alas ! has ever cast

    Its shadow here : —

Where long the gaping crowd may gaze

Till weariness their wonder wear

    To common thought,

And Truth, worn out by length of days,

Is varnished into falsehood fair,

    Let such be sought.

More favoured tree that, night and day,
By morn and twilight's beam of gold,
    Art doomed to wave
Where travellers pause awhile and say,
" Here sleeps a sage and warrior bold —
    'Tis HAVELOCK's grave ! "

Not stony thou ; untaught, unbid ;
Thy ceaseless labour to declare
    To passers-by,
Whose sacred ashes here are hid,
Where Truth shall Time itself outwear,
    And death shall die.

When, of Ambition's army, they
Who sought with restless zeal, and found,
    A crown below,
Have passed from Honour's scroll away,
With every withered wreath that bound
    Each mortal brow,

Still, living page that nigh the throne
Of Paradise, no time can dim,
    Or flame consume,
His name shall cease not to be known
On thee : a fadeless crown for him
    Shall ever bloom.

Rest, warrior, rest ! thy victory won,—
Thy marches and thy conflicts o'er,—
    Thy country blest :
Nor pestilence, nor midday sun
On Indian plain, shall smite thee more :
    Rest, warrior, rest !

So rests his soul where conflicts cease,
In robes of stainless white arrayed,
    From every care :
The palms of Victory and peace,
Of ever vernal trees, the shade,
    Thrice welcome there !

THE DEPARTED SABBATH.

A SABBATH gone—for ever gone !
Another's sun may not arise
Ere I unclose these wond'ring eyes
Upon the resurrection morn ;—

Ere I behold the " great white throne"
On which He sits, before whose face
The Heaven and Earth can find no place,
But man must give account alone :

No sheltering hill—no secret cave,
To hide him from that scene, is there,—
No ocean, in whose depths Despair
Itself could smile to find a grave ;

No tempest-laden clouds, whose gloom
Lends a dark sanction to his flight
Who fain would steal, by dead of night,
Back to the silence of the tomb.—

Ere I behold, as far as ken
Can wander through unbounded space,
The countless hosts redeeming grace
Has ransomed of the sons of men;—

See, beautiful in white array
Each heir of heavenly glory stand,
Or stoop to kiss the piercèd hand
Which gives a golden crown away.

A Sabbath gone—for ever gone!
Another's sun may not arise
Ere I unclose these wond'ring eyes
Upon the resurrection morn.

NOTES.

NOTES.

Page 17, line 10.

Whose streets of gold as glass transparent shine.

" And the street of the city was pure gold, as it were transparent glass."— *Rev.* xxi. 21.

Page 17, line 15.

To seraph harps refined, and ever tuned.

" Then crowned again their golden harps they took,
    Harps ever tuned."

MILTON, *Paradise Lost*, b. iii. l. 365.

Page 19, line 3.

*The cloud that always must conceal that spot
And Heaven's high-road without me.*

" Jesus saith unto him, I am the way."—*John*, xiv. 6.

Page 19, line 8.

Whence rose a sound as, swifter than their flow,
O'er many waters floats.

" And his feet like unto fine brass, as if they burned in a furnace ; and his voice as the sound of many waters."—*Rev.* i. 15.

Page 21, line 8.

Was sorrow e'er like His deep sorrow seen,
Whom Heaven hath sore afflicted ?

" Is it nothing to you, all ye that pass by? behold and see if there be any sorrow like unto my sorrow, which is done unto me, wherewith the Lord hath afflicted me in the day of his fierce anger."— *Lam.* i. 12.

Page 21, line 19.

The crown He wore
From brier to myrtle grown of living bloom :
Each hill broke forth in singing, and the trees
Clapped all their hands.

" Instead of the thorn shall come up the fir-tree, and instead of the brier shall come up the myrtle tree."—*Isa.* lv. 13.

" For ye shall go out with joy, and be led forth with peace : the mountains and the hills shall break forth before you into singing, and all the trees of the field shall clap their hands."— *Isa.* lv. 12.

Page 38, line 3.

Clouds like the wings of angels.

" Holy thoughts, like stars, arise,
    Its clouds are angels' wings."
        LONGFELLOW, *Prelude to Voices of the Night.*

Page 63, line 10.

More noble he, &c.   Aristides, named " the Just."

Page 79, line 5.

And there are gatherings, chill, forlorn, on Arvon's sea-damp sand.

" On dreary Arvon's shore they lie."—GRAY's *Bard.*

London :— Printed by G. BARCLAY, Castle St. Leicester Sq.

June 1860.

𝔚orks 𝔓ublished

BY

HATCHARD AND CO.

187 PICCADILLY, LONDON, W.

ABERNETHY, Dr. J.—Memoirs of John Abernethy, F.R.S. With a View of his Lectures, Writings, and Character, and Documents relating to his Religious Views, &c. By GEORGE MACIL-WAIN, F.R.C.S. Third Edition, with two Portraits. 8vo. cloth, 10s. 6d.

"We recommend it as replete with interest and instruction."—*Record.*

ALFORD, Rev. W.—The Old and New Testament Dispensations compared; showing in what respects they differ; what things are peculiar to the former; and what are common to both. By WALTER ALFORD, M.A. Perpetual Curate of Muchelney, Somerset. Crown 8vo. cloth. 12s.

"Mr. Alford has bestowed a great deal of labour on this volume, and executed his design in a learned and pious manner. He is properly sensible of the intimate connexion of the two Testaments, both as to the inspiring power which pervades them, the substantial oneness of their design, and the continuity of divine operation from the commencement of the one to the close of the other. We recommend the work as a useful addition to an important department of theology."—JOURNAL SACRED LITERATURE.

"This is a book of great value on a subject of far higher importance than at first view might appear. The work, it will be seen, necessarily embraces a vast variety of subjects. It is certainly admirably adapted to the wants and requirements of theological students in the present day. We cordially recommend the entire volume. After the work has been carefully read through, as it deserves to be, it is well calculated for standing usefulness as a book of reference."—RECORD.

ANDERSON, Rev. R.—A Practical Exposition of the Gospel of St. John. By the late Rev. ROBERT ANDERSON, Perpetual Curate of Trinity Chapel, Brighton. 2 vols. 12mo. cloth, 14s.

—— Ten Discourses on the Communion Office of the Church of England. With an Appendix. Second Edition. 12mo. cloth, 7s.

ANLEY, Miss C.—Earlswood: a Tale for the Times. By CHARLOTTE ANLEY. Second Thousand. Fcap. cloth, 7s. 6d.

"A pleasing and gracefully written tale, detailing the process by which persons of piety are sometimes perverted to Romish error."—*English Review.*
"This tale is singularly well conceived."—*Evangelical Magazine.*
"We can recommend it with confidence."—*Christian Times.*

—— Miriam; or, the Power of Truth. A Jewish Tale. Tenth Edition, with a Portrait. Fcap. cloth, 6s.

BACON, Rev. H. B.—Lectures for the Use of Sick Persons. By the Rev. H. B. BACON, M.A. Fcap. cloth, 4s. 6d.

"The Lectures possess two very great recommendations. First,—they are brief, concise, and to the point; and secondly,—the language is plain, free from ambiguity, and scriptural, &c. &c. It may be very profitably meditated upon by the sick; and young clergymen will not lay it down after perusal without having derived some instruction."—*Christian Guardian.*

Bible Stories, selected from the Old and New Testament, familiarised for the Use of Children; in Portions. By the Author of "Questions on the Epistles," &c. Third Edition. 2 vols. 18mo. half-bound, each 2s. 6d.

BIDDULPH, Rev. T. — The Young Churchman Armed. A Catechism for Junior Members of the Church of England. By the late Rev. THEOPHILUS BIDDULPH, A.M. Third Edition. 18mo. cloth, 1s.

BIRD, Rev. C. S.—Romanism Unknown to Primitive Christianity. The substance of Lectures delivered in the Parish Church of Gainsborough. By the Rev. C. S. BIRD, M.A. F.L.S. Chancellor of Lincoln, and late Fellow of Trinity College, Cambridge. Fcap. cl. 5s.

—— For Ever ; and other Devotional Poems, particularly Hymns adapted to the Earlier Psalms. Second Edition. 32mo. silk, 2s. 6d.

BLUNT, Rev. H. — Posthumous Sermons. By the late Rev. HENRY BLUNT, M.A. Rector of Streatham, Surrey. Third Edition, with a Portrait. 3 vols. 12mo. cloth, each 6s.

—— A Family Exposition of the Pentateuch. Fourth Edition. 3 vols. 12mo. cloth, each 6s.

—— Nine Lectures upon the History of Saint Peter. Nineteenth Edition. 12mo. cloth, 4s. 6d.

—— Eight Lectures on the History of Jacob. Seventeenth Edition. 12mo. cloth, 4s. 6d.

—— Twelve Lectures on the History of Abraham. Thirteenth Edition. 12mo. cloth, 5s. 6d.

—— Lectures on the History of Saint Paul. Eleventh Edition. 2 Parts. 12mo. cloth, each 5s. 6d.

—— Lectures on the History of our Lord and Saviour Jesus Christ. Twelfth Edition. 3 Parts. 12mo. cloth, each 5s. 6d.

—— Discourses upon some of the Doctrinal Articles of the Church of England. Ninth Edition. 12mo. cloth, 5s. 6d.

—— Sermons preached in Trinity Church, Chelsea. Seventh Edition. 12mo. cloth, 6s.

—— A Practical Exposition of the Epistles to the Seven Churches of Asia. Fifth Edition. 12mo. cloth, 5s. 6d.

—— Lectures on the History of Elisha. Fifth Edition. 12mo. cloth, 5s. 6d.

BOSWELL, Rev. M.—Baptism, considered in its Nature and Effects. With an Appendix, containing an Explanation of those Passages of Holy Scripture which relate to the subject. By the REV. MARTIN BOSWELL, M.A. formerly Fellow of Clare College, Cambridge. Fcap. cloth, 2*s*.

Bow in the Cloud: a Memoir of M. E. H. By her SISTER, Author of "Ellen Mordaunt." Fcap. cloth, 3*s*. 6*d*.

"A simple, but touching biography. It records the trials and the consolations of one whose father died after a lingering illness, shortly before the period of her own dissolution; and whose mother survived this shock for a few months only. The experience of sorrow is thus sketched, under no ordinary circumstances, by the only surviving member of the family. There is nothing of maudlin sentimentalism in the book; it conveys some weighty lessons to the Christian reader."—*Liverpool Courier.*

BRADLEY, Rev. A.—Sermons, chiefly on Character: preached at Hale, Surrey. By the Rev. ARTHUR BRADLEY, M.A. Perpetual Curate of Hale, and Michel Fellow of Queen's College, Oxford. Fcap. cloth, 5*s*.

BRADLEY, Rev. C.—Sermons, preached chiefly at the Celebration of the Lord's Supper. By the Rev. CHARLES BRADLEY, Vicar of Glasbury, Brecknockshire. Third Edition. 8vo. cloth, 10*s*. 6*d*.

—— Practical Sermons for every Sunday and Principal Holyday in the Year. Fourth Edition. Complete in 1 vol. 8vo. cloth, 12*s*.

—— Sermons preached in the Parish Church of Glasbury, Brecknockshire, and St. James's Chapel, Clapham, Surrey. Ninth Edition. In 1 vol. 8vo. cloth, 10*s*. 6*d*.

—— Sermons on some of the Trials, Duties, and Encouragements of the Christian Life. Second Edition. 8vo. cloth, 10*s*. 6*d*.

—— Sunday Questions for Families and the Junior Classes in Schools. 18mo. cloth, 1*s*.

BURTT, J.—Exempla Necessaria; or, Elementary Latin Exercises on all the Parts of Speech, and the Substance of Syntax; containing English Words and Sentences to be turned into Latin, Latin into English, and numerous Examination Questions to be entered on with the Accidence. With an Introduction. By J. BURTT, Teacher of Latin, &c. Third Edition, much enlarged. 18mo. cloth, 2*s*. 6*d*.

Calling and Responsibilities of a Governess. By AMICA. Fcap. cloth, 3*s*.

CANTERBURY, Archbishop of.—Practical Reflections on Select Passages of the New Testament. By JOHN BIRD SUMNER, D.D., Lord Archbishop of Canterbury. Chiefly compiled from Expository Lectures on the Gospels and Epistles, by the same Author. Post 8vo. cloth, 5s. 6d.

—— A Practical Exposition of the New Testament, in the form of Lectures, intended to assist the practice of Domestic Instruction and Devotion. 9 vols. 8vo. cloth (each volume being a separate work), price 9s. each.

—— Christian Charity; its Obligations and Objects, with reference to the present state of Society. In a series of Sermons. Second Edition. 8vo. cloth, 9s.; or 12mo. 6s.

—— Apostolical Preaching Considered, in an Examination of St. Paul's Epistles. Also, Four Sermons on Subjects relating to the Christian Ministry, and preached on different occasions. Ninth Edition, enlarged, 8vo. cloth, 10s. 6d.

—— The Evidences of Christianity, derived from its Nature and Reception. Seventh Edition, 8vo. cloth, 10s. 6d.; or fcap. 3s.

—— A Series of Sermons on the Christian Faith and Character. Eighth Edition, 8vo. cloth, 10s. 6d.; or 12mo. 6s.

—— A Treatise on the Records of the Creation, and on the Moral Attributes of the Creator. Sixth Edition, 8vo. cloth, 10s. 6d.

CHAMBERS, Miss A.—Comfort in Sleepless Nights. Passages selected by ANNE CHAMBERS. Royal 8vo. (large type) cloth, 3s. 6d.

Christ our Example. By the Author of "The Listener." Eighth Edition. Fcap. cloth, 5s.
Contents.—1. In the Object of Life—2. In the Rule of Life—3. In his Intercourse with the World—4. In the Condition of Life—5. In his Sorrows—6. In his Joys—7. In his Death.

Christian Observer, conducted by Members of the Established Church. Published monthly, price 1s. 6d.

Christian Sympathy; a Collection of Letters addressed to Mourners. 32mo. cloth, gilt edges, 2*s.* 6*d.*

CHURTON, Rev. H. B. W.—Thoughts on the Land of the Morning; a Record of Two Visits to Palestine, 1849–50. By H. B. WHITAKER CHURTON, M.A. Vicar of Icklesham, Sussex, Chaplain to the Lord Bishop of Chichester, and late Preacher of the Charter-house. Second Edition, corrected and enlarged. Crown 8vo. with numerous illustrations, cloth, 10*s.* 6*d.*

CLOSE, Dean.—Miscellaneous Sermons, preached at Cheltenham. By the Very Rev. F. CLOSE, D.D. Dean of Carlisle. Second Edition. 2 vols. 8vo. boards, 21*s.*

Common Sense for Housemaids. By A LADY. Third Edition, corrected. 12mo. 1*s.*

Companion to the Book of Common Prayer of the United Church of England and Ireland. 24mo. cloth, 2*s.* 6*d.*

Consistency. By CHARLOTTE ELIZABETH. Sixth Edition. 18mo. boards, 2*s.* 6*d.*

Constance and Edith; or, Incidents of Home Life. By a CLERGYMAN'S WIFE. Fcap. cloth, 4*s.* 6*d.*

"This is one of those simple quiet tales of English domestic life which afford pleasure to youthful readers; its tone is religious and moral, lessons being also conveyed on useful practical points in regard to behaviour and conduct. It is a tale that may be safely and with advantage put into the hands of children."—*Literary Gazette.*

"A well-intentioned and pleasant tale, really consisting of 'Incidents of Home Life.'"—*Spectator.*

"The story is sufficiently varied in its incidents to sustain the attention of the readers throughout."—*Morning Post.*

"This is a pleasing book for young people, and, as such, we are glad to recommend it."—*Church of England Magazine.*

"This interesting tale will become a great favourite with both parents and children."—*Morning Herald.*

COURTENAY, Bishop.—The Future States, their Evidences and Nature : considered on Principles Physical, Moral, and Scriptural, with the Design of showing the Value of Gospel Revelation. By the Right Rev. REGINALD COURTENAY, D.D. Lord Bishop of Kingston, Jamaica. 8vo. cloth, 6*s.*

COUTTS, Miss BURDETT.—A Summary Account of Prizes for Common Things, offered and awarded by Miss Burdett Coutts at the Whitelands Training Institution. Third Edition, greatly enlarged, 8vo. cloth, 1*s.* 6*d.*

CREWDSON, Mrs.—Lays of the Reformation and other Lyrics, Scriptural and Miscellaneous. By JANE CREWDSON, Author of "The Singer of Eisenach," "Aunt Jane's Verses for Children, &c. Fcap. cloth, 5s.

"We have read these Poems with much pleasure ourselves, and we doubt not that our readers will enjoy their high religious tone, their rapid but faithful picturesqueness, their faultless music, and their many delicate delineations."—*Literary Gazette.*

"The verse is sonorous rather than sinewy, frequently, however, pleasing rather than otherwise. The Authoress has good aspirations, and some tenderness of feeling."—*Athenæum.*

"This little volume contains some very sweet verses and noble thoughts."—*Morning Herald.*

"Spirited stanzas in praise of Wycliffe, Luther, and others."—*Clerical Journal.*

CRUDEN, A.—A complete Concordance to the Holy Scriptures of the Old and New Testament; or, A Dictionary and Alphabetical Index to the Bible. In Two Parts. To which is added, A Concordance to the Apocrypha. By ALEXANDER CRUDEN, M.A. The Ninth Edition. With a Life of the Author, by ALEXANDER CHALMERS, F.S.A. 4to. boards, 1l. 1s.

CUNNINGHAM, Rev. J. W.—Sermons. By the Rev. J. W. CUNNINGHAM, A.M. Vicar of Harrow, and late Fellow of St. John's College, Cambridge. Fifth Edition. 2 vols. 8vo. bds. 1l. 1s.

——— Six Lectures on the Book of Jonah. Fcap. boards, 3s.

——— The Velvet Cushion. Eleventh Edition. Fcap. boards, 5s.

DRUMMOND, H.—Social Duties on Christian Principles. By the late HENRY DRUMMOND, Esq. M.P. Fifth Edition. Fcap. cloth, 4s.

EDELMAN, Rev. W.—Sermons on the History of Joseph. Preached in the Parish Church of St. Mary, Wimbledon. By the Rev. W. EDELMAN, Perpetual Curate of Merton. 12mo. cloth, 5s.

——— The Family Pastor; or, Short Sermons for Family Reading. 12mo. cloth, 3s. 6d.

EDMUNDS, Rev. J.—The Seven Sayings of Christ on the Cross. Seven Lent Lectures. To which is prefixed, a Gospel Harmony of the Passion of our Lord and Saviour Jesus Christ. With Explanatory Notes. By the Rev. JOHN EDMUNDS, M.A. formerly Fellow of the University of Durham. Fcap. cloth, 3s. 6d.

EDMUNDS, Rev. J.

—— Sermons, preached for the most part in a Country Church in the Diocese of Durham. Second Series. Fcap. cloth, 5s. 6d.

"The Sermons contained in this volume are generally sound and eminently practical, and admirably adapted for the purpose for which they are published—to be read in families to children and servants on the Sunday evening."—*John Bull.*

Eighteen Maxims of Neatness and Order. To which is prefixed an Introduction by THERESA TIDY. Twenty-fourth Edition. 18mo. sewed, 6d.

Ethel Woodville; or, Woman's Ministry. A Tale for the Times. 2 vols. fcap. cloth, 12s.

"'Ethel Woodville' is a tale told by a graceful and a pious pen. Its moral is, that no woman can expect happiness if she be united to a man not having the fear of God. The character of the heroine is finely and tenderly drawn, and the whole progress of the story moves gracefully and gently. There is no turmoil, no exciting scenes; and yet it may be read without weariness, but certainly not without profit."—THE CRITIC.

"A clever story; we can recommend it as being considerably above the common level of its kind."—LITERARY GAZETTE.

Far off: Part I.; or Asia Described. With Anecdotes and numerous Illustrations. By the Author of "Peep of Day," &c. Eighteenth Thousand. Fcap. cloth, 4s. 6d.

"We have sometimes met clergymen who are in the habit of endeavouring to promote the Missionary cause in their parishes, who would be thankful for such a little book as this. It seems to us just the sort of book that might be read out to a class of young persons, either in National Schools or otherwise, and which would be certain to interest them exceedingly."—*English Review.*

—— Part II.; or, Australia, Africa, and America Described. With Anecdotes, and numerous Illustrations. Twelfth Thousand. Fcap. cloth, 4s. 6d.

FAWCETT, Rev. J.—An Exposition of the Gospel according to St. John. By the Rev. JOHN FAWCETT, M.A. late Incumbent of St. Cuthbert's, Carlisle. 3 vols. 8vo. cloth, 21s.

—— An Exposition of the Acts of the Apostles. 3 vols. 8vo. cloth, 24s.

—— Christian Life; or, the Principles and Practice which distinguish the Genuine Christian. Illustrated in Thirty Discourses. 8vo. cloth, 7s.

FENELON.—Extracts from the Religious Works of Fenelon, Archbishop of Cambray. Translated from the Original French by Miss MARSHALL. Eleventh Edition, with a Portrait. Fcap. cloth, 5s.

FINCHER, J. — The Achievements of Prayer.
Selected exclusively from the Holy Scriptures. By the late JOSEPH
FINCHER, Esq. With a Testimony to the Work by the late James Mont-
gomery. Third Edition. 12mo. cloth, 6s.

FORSYTH, Rev. J. H.—Sermons by the late Rev.
JOHN HAMILTON FORSYTH, M.A. Curate of Weston-super-Mare, and
afterwards Minister of Dowry Chapel, Clifton, Domestic Chaplain to the
Marquis of Thomond. With a Memoir of the Author, by the Rev.
EDWARD WILSON, M.A. Vicar of Nocton, Lincolnshire. Third Edition.
8vo. cloth, with Portrait, 10s. 6d.

"The character of Mr. Forsyth is one which we greatly admire," &c.— *Christian
Observer.*

GARBETT, Archdeacon. — Christ on Earth, in Heaven, and on the Judgment-seat. By the Ven. JAMES GARBETT, M.A.
Archdeacon of Chichester. 2 vols. 12mo. cloth, 12s.

"No one can read these volumes without great delight and profit."— *Christian
Observer.*

—— Parochial Sermons. 2 vols. 8vo. cloth,
each 12s.

—— Christ as Prophet, Priest, and King; being a
Vindication of the Church of England from Theological Novelties. In
Eight Lectures, preached before the University of Oxford, at Canon
Bampton's Lecture, 1842. 2 vols. 8vo. cloth 1l. 4s.

—— The Beatitudes of the Mount. In Seventeen
Sermons. 12mo. cloth, 7s.

"There is a depth and a solidity in these discourses, which favourably distinguish
them from so many of the superficial productions with which the press is teeming.
The reader cannot but feel that he has something worth thinking of presented to him;
and the more he ponders them the greater will be his profit."—*Church of England
Magazine.*

GIBBON, E. — The History of the Decline and Fall
of the Roman Empire. By EDWARD GIBBON, Esq. New Edition.
8 vols. 8vo. cloth, 3l.

GIBSON, Bishop.—The Sacrament of the Lord's
Supper Explained; or, the Things to be known and done to make a
worthy Communicant. With suitable Prayers and Meditations. By
EDMUND GIBSON, D.D. late Lord Bishop of London. New Edition,
Fcap. cloth, 2s. 6d.

—— Family Devotion; or, an Exhortation to
Morning and Evening Prayer in Families: with two Forms of Prayer,
suited to those two Seasons, and also fitted for the use of one Person in
Private, &c. (Reprinted from the Eighteenth Edition.) Fcap. cloth, 2s.

A 2

The Gipsies. Dedicated, by permission, to JAMES CRABB, the Gipsies' Friend. Fcap. cloth, 4*s*. 6*d*.

GOODE, Rev. F.—The Better Covenant practically Considered, from Heb. viii. 6, 10–12; with a Supplement on Philip. ii. 12, 13, and Notes. By the late Rev. F. GOODE, M.A. Fifth Edition. To which is added, A Sermon on Jer. xxxi. 31–34. Fcap. cloth, 7*s*.

GOODE, Dean.—The Nature of Christ's Presence in the Eucharist; or, the True Doctrine of the Real Presence Vindicated; in opposition to the fictitious Real Presence asserted by Archdeacon Denison, Mr. (late Archdeacon) Wilberforce, and Dr. Pusey: with full proof of the real character of the attempt made by those authors to represent their doctrine as that of the Church of England and her divines. By the Very Rev. WILLIAM GOODE, D.D. F.S.A. Dean of Ripon. 2 vols. 8vo. cloth, 24*s*.

—— Aid for Determining some Disputed Points in the Ceremonial of the Church of England. Second Edition, 8vo. cloth, 4*s*.

—— A Vindication of the Doctrine of the Church of England on the Validity of the Orders of the Scotch and Foreign Non-Episcopal Churches. 8vo. cloth, 5*s*.

—— The Doctrine of the Church of England as to the Effects of Baptism in the case of Infants. With an Appendix, containing the Baptismal Services of Luther and the Nuremberg and Cologne Liturgies. Second Edition. 8vo. cloth, 15*s*.

The Gospel of Other Days; or, Thoughts on Old and New Testament Scriptures. By the Author of " Seed Time and Harvest." 18mo. cloth, 2*s*.

" We heartily welcome the little book . . . . As a sound and eminently practical compression of a great subject into a very small compass, we can heartily recommend it."—*Bickersteth's Weekly Visitor.*

GRAGLIA, C.—A Pocket Dictionary of the Italian and English Languages. By C. GRAGLIA. Square 18mo. bound, 4*s*. 6*d*.

GRAY, Mrs. H.—History of Rome for Young Persons. With numerous Wood Engravings. Second Edition, corrected. By Mrs. HAMILTON GRAY. 1 vol. 12mo. cloth, 8*s*.

" A very ingenious attempt to bring the recent discoveries of the critical school into working competition with the miserable Goldsmiths and Pinnocks of our youth."—*Christian Remembrancer.*

" The clear, lively, and pleasing style of narration is admirably calculated to awaken and sustain the attention."—*Athenæum.*

GRAY, Mrs. H.

—— Emperors of Rome from Augustus to Constantine: being a Continuation of the History of Rome. 1 vol. 12mo. with Illustrations, 8*s*.

" So many applications are made to us for histories suited to a period of life when the mind is beginning to develope its power, and to find satisfaction in connecting the past with the present and the future in human affairs, that we are induced to recommend these volumes, which, however widely circulated, have not half the circulation which they deserve. They are clearly written. They neither minister to childish imbecility, nor take for granted a measure of knowledge which cannot be lawfully expected of the young. They present the page of history as it really is—not a series of dry details, nor of gorgeous spectacles, but with enough of plain fact to instruct the understanding, and of romantic incident to kindle the sympathies and affections."—*Christian Observer.*

" We have no hesitation in saying, that this is one of the best histories of the Roman Empire for children and young people which has come under our notice. Mrs. Hamilton Gray has made herself acquainted with at least some of the more important ancient writers on the subject of which she treats, and also with the criticisms of Niebuhr and other modern investigators of Roman history."—*Athenæum.*

" It may be recommended as a clear, rapid, and well-arranged summary of facts, pointed by frequent but brief reflections. . . . The book is a very good compendium of the Imperial History, primarily designed for children, but useful for all."—*Spectator.*

" It would be an erroneous impression to convey of this volume, that it is written solely for schools and children. In reality it is an abridgment far more likely to be useful to grown-up persons, who can reflect upon the working of general laws, and make their own observations upon men and things. A striking characteristic of the book is the impartiality of its political tone, and its high moral feeling."—*Examiner.*

—— The History of Etruria. Part I. Tarchun and his Times. From the Foundation of Tarquinia to the Foundation of Rome. Part II. From the Foundation of Rome to the General Peace of Anno Tarquiniensis, 839, B.C. 348. 2 vols. post 8vo. cloth, each 12*s*.

" A work which we strongly recommend as certain to afford pleasure and profit to every reader."—*Athenæum.*

—— Tour to the Sepulchres of Etruria in 1839. Third Edition. With numerous Illustrations, post 8vo. cloth, 1*l*. 1*s*.

" Mrs. Gray has won an honourable place in the large assembly of modern female writers."—*Quarterly Review.*

" We warmly recommend Mrs. Gray's most useful and interesting volume."—*Edinburgh Review.*

GRAY, Miss A. T.—The Twin Pupils; or, Education at Home. A Tale addressed to the Young. By ANN THOMSON GRAY. Fcap. cloth, 7*s*. 6*d*.

" The story is well planned, well varied, and well written."—*Spectator.*

" More sound principles and useful practical remarks we have not lately met in any work on the much-treated subject of education. The book is written with liveliness as well as good sense."—*Literary Gazette.*

" A volume of excellent tendency, which may be put with safety and advantage into the hands of well-educated young people."—*Evangelical Magazine.*

GRIFFITH, Rev. T.—The Spiritual Life. By the Rev. THOMAS GRIFFITH, A.M. Minister of Ram's Episcopal Chapel, Homerton. Eighth Edition. Fcap. cloth, 4*s*.

GRIFFITH, Rev. T.

—— Sermons preached in St. James's Chapel, Ryde. Second Edition. Fcap. cloth, 5s.

—— Live while you Live. Seventh Edition. 18mo. cloth, 1s. 6d.

—— The Lord's Prayer: contemplated as the Expression of the Primary Elements of Devoutness. Second Edition. Fcap. cloth, 2s.

—— The Lord's Supper: its Nature, Requirements, Benefits. Third Edition. Fcap. cloth, 1s. 6d.

—— Confirmation, and the Baptismal Vow for Catechumens, Communicants, Parents, and Sponsors; with Practical Helps for Catechumens. Fourth Edition. Fcap. cloth, 2s.

—— Confirmation: its Object, Importance, and Benefit; with Practical Helps for those about to be Confirmed. Sixth Edition. · Price 4d. or 3s. 6d. per doz.

GRIMSTON, Hon. Miss.—Arrangement of the Common Prayer-Book and Lessons. Dedicated, by Permission, to Her Majesty.

The peculiar advantage of this arrangement consists in having the entire Morning and Evening Services printed in a clear type, in two portable volumes, one for the Morning and the other for the Evening.

Royal 32mo. morocco, elegant £1 4 0		
Ditto plain 1 1 0		
Ditto calf, gilt leaves 0 16 0		

HANKINSON, Rev. T. E. — Poems. By THOMAS EDWARDS HANKINSON, M.A. late of Corpus Christi College, Cambridge, and Minister of St. Matthew's Chapel, Denmark Hill. Edited by his Brothers. Fifth Edition. Fcap. cloth, 7s.

—— Sermons. 8vo. cloth, 10s. 6d.

HARE, Rev. A. W.—Sermons to a Country Congregation. By AUGUSTUS WILLIAM HARE, A.M. late Fellow of New College, and Rector of Alton Barnes. Eighth Edition. 2 vols. 12mo. cloth, 14s.

"They are, in truth, as appears to us, compositions of very rare merit, and realise a notion we have always entertained, that a sermon for our rural congregations there somewhere was, if it could be hit off, which in language should be familiar without being plain, and in matter solid without being abstruse."—*Quarterly Review*.

HASTINGS, Rev. H. J.—Parochial Sermons, from
Trinity to Advent. By HENRY JAMES HASTINGS, M.A. Honorary Canon
of Worcester, Rural Dean, Rector of Martley, Worcestershire. 8vo.
cloth, 12*s.*

HATCHARD, Rev. T. G.—The Floweret Gathered;
a Brief Memoir of a Departed Daughter. By T. GOODWIN HATCHARD,
M.A. Rector of St. Nicholas, Guildford. Third Thousand. Square
16mo. 1*s.*

"This is an account of one of the lambs of Christ's fold, who exhibited the truest
simplicity and natural character of a child, united to unwavering trust in and love to
that Saviour, who took her early to himself. It is calculated both to interest, and, we
trust, greatly to profit, our young friends, as a pattern of early piety."—*Church of England
Sunday-school Monthly Magazine for Teachers.*

" No one can rise from the perusal of this little volume without feeling deeply inter-
ested in the lovely character of the dear Addie."—*Jewish Intelligence.*

" This is a touching little narrative for the young. Few will read it without a full
heart, and the shedding of a tear of sweet sympathy with ' The Floweret Gathered.'"—
Children's Jewish Advocate.

—— Thanksgiving; or, The Wave-Offering and
the Heave-Offering. A Harvest Sermon preached in Havant Church
on Sunday, August 20, 1854. 8vo. price 6*d.*

—— The German Tree; or, a Moral for the
Young. Price 1*s.*

—— Feed My Lambs: a Lecture for Children in
Words of One Syllable; to which is added a Hymn. Seventh Thousand.
32mo. 3*d.*; or 2*s.* 6*d.* per dozen.

—— Food for my Flock: being Sermons delivered
in the Parish Church of Havant, Hants. Fcap. cloth, 5*s.* 6*d.*

"These Sermons are marked by unaffected piety, great clearness of exposition, and a
direct plainness of style and purpose which render them pre-eminently practical."—
Britannia.

"A set of plain, spirited discourses, which are not unlikely to disturb the repose of
the drowsy, and to send home simple truths to the hearts that heed them. The Sermons
are, besides, scriptural in their doctrinal views, charitable in temper, unpolemical,
rather asserting the truth than contending for it."—*Christian Observer.*

HATHERELL, Rev. Dr.—The Signs of the Second
Advent of our Blessed Lord, collected from the words of Jesus and ap-
plied to our own times. In Twelve Sermons, preached during the season
of Advent, in the years 1856 and 1857, in the Church of St. James, West-
end, Southampton. By JAMES WILLIAMS HATHERELL, D.D. Incumbent.
12mo. cloth, 5*s.*

HEPPE, Dr. — The Reformers of England and Germany in the Sixteenth Century; their Intercourse and Correspondence. A Historical Sketch, including valuable Original Documents. By Dr. HEPPE, of Marburg, Author of " A History of Protestantism," &c. Translated, with additions, including hitherto unpublished letters from Martin Luther and Justus Jonas to Thomas Cromwell. By the Rev. Hermann Schmettau and Rev. B. Harris Cowper. Fcap. cloth, 2s. 6d.

" This is a well-informed and beautiful volume, presenting a valuable selection of historic facts touching great men, the instruments of producing a great revolution in human affairs."—BRITISH BANNER.

HEY, Mrs. — The Holy Places, a series of Sonnets; and other Poems. By REBECCA HEY, Author of "The Moral of Flowers," "The Spirit of the Woods," "Recollections of the Lakes," &c. &c. Fcap. cloth, 5s.

" ' The Holy Places and other Poems' are of no common order ; the thoughts being finely conceived, and the expression very perfect. The Sonnets deserve to be generally known."—CLERICAL JOURNAL.

" Chaste, sweet, and musical are these poems. There is a spirit of natural poetry in every throb of her muse, and one can hardly rise from a perusal of this little volume without having imbibed pleasure and instruction."—CRITIC.

" There is vigour and freshness about these poems, combined with much real earnestness of purpose."—BELL'S MESSENGER.

" These poems are conceived in an eminently pious spirit, and marked by a very fair amount of literary ability. The proceeds of the work are to be devoted to the aid of the Special Missions in India."—THE STAR.

Hints on Early Education and Nursery Discipline. Sixteenth Edition. 12mo. cloth, 3s. 6d.

Hints for Reflection. Compiled from various Authors. Third Edition. 32mo. cloth, 2s.

HODGSON, Rev. C. — Family Prayers for One Month. By various Clergymen. Arranged and Edited by the Rev. CHARLES HODGSON, M.A. Rector of Barton-le-Street, Yorkshire. Abridged Edition. To which have been added, Prayers for Particular Seasons.

Amongst the Contributors are His Grace the Archbishop of Canterbury, the late Rev. Chancellor Raikes, the Ven. Archdeacon Sandford, the late Rev. J. Haldane Stewart, Rev. Charles Bridges, Rev. C. A. Thurlow, the late Rev. E. Bickersteth, &c. &c. Fcap. cloth, 3s. 6d.

Holidays at Lynmere; or, Conversations on the Miracles of our Lord. By a LADY. Edited by the Rev. CHARLES F. MACKENZIE, M.A. Fellow of Caius College, Cambridge. 18mo. cloth, 2s.

HOPE, Dr.—Memoirs of the late James Hope, M.D.
Physician to St. George's Hospital, &c. &c. By Mrs. HOPE. To which
are added, Remarks on Classical Education, by Dr. HOPE. And
Letters from a Senior to a Junior Physician, by Dr. BURDER. The
whole edited by KLEIN GRANT, M.D. &c. &c. Fourth Edition. Post
8vo. cloth, 7s.

" The general, as well as the medical reader, will find this a most interesting and
instructive volume."—*Gentleman's Magazine.*
" A very interesting memoir to every class of readers."—*Christian Observer.*

HUME and SMOLLETT.—The History of England,
from the Invasion of Julius Cæsar to the Death of George the Second.
By D. HUME and T. SMOLLETT. 10 vols. 8vo. cloth, 4l.

The Interrogator; or, Universal Ancient History,
in Questions and Answers. By a LADY. 12mo. roan, 5s.

JACKSON, Rev. F.—Sermons. By the Rev. FRE-
DERIC JACKSON, Incumbent of Parson Drove, Isle of Ely. 2 vols. fcap.
cloth, each 5s.

" Discourses addressed to a village congregation. The chief aim of the preacher has
been to enforce practical conclusions for the guidance of the humblest, from some of the
most striking events or sentiments of Scripture. The style is plain and forcible."—
Spectator.

JEWSBURY, Miss M. J.—Letters to the Young.
By MARIA JANE JEWSBURY. Fifth Edition. Fcap. cloth, 5s.

Light in the Dwelling; or, a Harmony of the Four
Gospels, with very Short and Simple Remarks adapted to Reading at
Family Prayers, and arranged in 365 sections, for every day of the year.
By the Author of " The Peep of Day," " Line upon Line," &c. Revised
and Corrected by a Clergyman of the Church of England. Eighteenth
Thousand. Post 8vo. cloth, 8s. ; or in 8vo. large type, 10s.

Line upon Line; or, a Second Series of the Earliest
Religious Instruction the Infant Mind is capable of receiving ; with
Verses illustrative of the Subjects. By the Author of " The Peep of
Day," &c. Part I. Eighty-third Thousand. Part II. Seventy-third
Thousand. 18mo. cloth, each 2s. 6d.

LITTON, Rev. E. A. — The Mosaic Dispensation
considered as Introductory to Christianity. Eight Sermons preached
before the University of Oxford, at the Bampton Lecture for 1856. By
the Rev. EDWARD ARTHUR LITTON, M.A., late Fellow of Oriel College.
8vo. cloth, 10s. 6d.

" We most earnestly direct the deep and serious attention of undergraduates at our
universities, and theological students generally, to these weighty and important
lectures."—*Record.*

M'NEILE, Rev. Dr.—Lectures on the Sympathies, Sufferings, and Resurrection of the Lord Jesus Christ, delivered in Liverpool during Passion Week and Easter Day. By HUGH M'NEILE, D.D., Hon. Canon of Chester, and Incumbent of St. Paul's Church, Prince's Park, Liverpool. Third Edition. 12mo. cloth, 4s. 6d.

MARRIOTT, Rev. H.—Sermons on the Character and Duties of Women. By the Rev. HARVEY MARRIOTT, Vicar of Loddiswell, and Chaplain to the Right Honourable Lord Kenyon. 12mo. cloth, 3s. 6d.

—— Four Courses of Practical Sermons.   8vo. each 10s. 6d.

MARSDEN, Rev. J. B.—The History of the Early Puritans; from the Reformation to the Opening of the Civil War in 1642. By J. B. MARSDEN, M.A. Second Edition. 8vo. cloth, 10s. 6d.

—— The History of the later Puritans; from the Opening of the Civil War in 1642, to the Ejection of the Non-conforming Clergy in 1662. Second Edition. 8vo. cloth, 10s. 6d.

MARSHALL, Miss.—Extracts from the Religious Works of Fénélon, Archbishop of Cambray. Translated from the Original French by Miss MARSHALL. Eleventh Edition, with a Portrait. Fcap. cloth, 5s.

MEEK, Rev. R.—The Mutual Recognition and Exalted Felicity of Glorified Saints. By the Rev. ROBERT MEEK, M.A. Rector of St. Michael, Sutton Bonnington, Notts. Sixth Edition. Fcap. cloth, 3s. 6d.

—— Passion Week; a Practical and Devotional Exposition of the Gospels and Epistles appointed for that Season, composed for the Closet and the Family. 12mo. boards, 4s.

MEREWEATHER, Rev. J. D.—Diary of a Working Clergyman in Australia and Tasmania, kept during the years 1850–1853; including his Return to England by way of Java, Singapore, Ceylon, and Egypt. By the Rev. JOHN DAVIES MEREWEATHER, B.A. Author of " Life on Board an Emigrant Ship." Fcap. cloth, 5s.

" We set great store by this volume, which abounds in interesting facts touching men and things, times and places, strange people and savage manners."—BRITISH BANNER.

" There is an unassuming spirit of religious faith and devotion to his Master's cause, which speaks well for the practical Christianity of the author; and so varied and amusing are the scenes and characters he discusses, that, blended with felicitous and original observations upon both, the combination results in one of the most attractive books of the present season."—JOHN BULL.

MERRY, W.—Futurity. By WILLIAM MERRY,
Esq. Sixth Edition. Fcap. cloth, 2s.

" This is an excellent, nay, a beautiful little work. We recommend it to the perusal
of doubters, and the enjoyment of believers—Christianity in its most affecting form to
unsophisticated and rightly constituted minds."—TIMES.

" He has written on a pleasing subject, and written well; and it is impossible to read
his little book without being the better for it. What is here advanced will assist the
reader in the very important work of setting his affections on the things above. The
nature of a future state of happiness, and its probable occupations, are treated in a
pious and thoughtful manner."—CLERICAL JOURNAL.

Mid-Day Thoughts for the Weary. Second Edition.
32mo. cloth, 1s. 6d.

More about Jesus; a Sequel to "Peep of Day."
By the same Author. Fifteenth Thousand. 18mo. cloth, with Illustrations by Harvey, 2s. 6d.

Near Home; or, the Countries of Europe described
to Children, with Anecdotes. By the Author of "Peep of Day,"
" Light in the Dwelling," &c. Illustrated with numerous Wood Engravings. Thirtieth Thousand. Fcap. cloth, 5s.

"It must be very interesting to children. Those to whom we have read passages,
taken at random, clap their little hands with delight."—*English Journal of Education.*

" A well-arranged and well-written book for children; compiled from the best writers
on the various countries, and full of sound and useful information, pleasantly conveyed
for the most part in the homely monosyllabic Saxon which children learn from their
mothers and nurses."—*Athenæum.*

New Manual of Devotions; containing Family and
Private Prayers, the Office for the Holy Communion, &c. 12mo. bd. 4s.

NEWNHAM, W.—A Tribute of Sympathy Addressed to Mourners. By W. NEWNHAM, Esq. Eleventh Edition.
Fcap. cloth, 5s.

Contents:—1. Indulgence of Grief.—2. Moderation of Grief.—3. Ex-
cessive Sorrow.—4. Advantages of Sorrow. —5. Self-examination.—6. Re-
signation.—7. Sources of Consolation.

—— Sunday-Evening Letters: a Correspondence
with an Intellectual Inquirer after Truth. Fcap. cloth, 5s.

Night of Toil; or, a Familiar Account of the
Labours of the First Missionaries in the South Sea Islands. By the
Author of " The Peep of Day," "Near Home," &c. Fourth Edition.
Fcap. cloth, 4s.

NIND, Rev. W.—Lecture-Sermons, preached in
a Country Parish Church. By WILLIAM NIND, M.A. late Fellow of
St. Peter's College, Cambridge, and Vicar of Cherry Hinton. Second
Series. 12mo. cloth, 6*s.*

"Sermons distinguished by brevity, good sense, and a plainness of manner and exposition which well adapt them for family perusal, especially as their style is neat and
simple, not bare."—*Spectator.*

"The many who have read the first volume of these sermons will welcome, no doubt
with joy, the appearance of the second. They are readable and preachable ; and those
of the second volume are even plainer and simpler than their predecessors. We recommend both volumes most heartily."—*English Review.*

NORTHESK, Countess of.—The Sheltering Vine.
Selections by the COUNTESS OF NORTHESK. With an Introduction by
the Very Rev. R. C. TRENCH, D.D., Dean of Westminster. Sixth
Thousand. 2 vols. small 8vo. cloth, 10*s.*

The object of this Work is to afford consolation under the various
trials of mind and body to which all are exposed, by a Selection of Texts
and Passages from Holy Scripture, and Extracts from Old and Modern
Authors, in Prose and Poetry, with a Selection of Prayers adapted to
the same.

—— A Selection of Prayers and Hymns, for the
Use of her Children. In Two Parts, 12mo. sewed, 1*s.*; cloth, 2*s.*

NUGENT'S Pocket Dictionary of the French and
English Languages. The Twenty-sixth Edition, revised by J. C. TARVER,
French Master, Eton, &c. Square 18mo. bound, 4*s.* 6*d.*

OAKLEY, Rev. C. E.—The English Bible, and its
History. A Lecture delivered in the School-room at Tortworth Court,
Gloucestershire, January 23, 1854. By the Rev. C. E. OAKLEY, B.A.
Rector of Wickwar, Gloucestershire, and Domestic Chaplain to the
Earl of Ducie. Fcap. cloth, 1*s.* 6*d.*

OXENDEN, Rev. A.—Fervent Prayer. By the
Rev. ASHTON OXENDEN, Rector of Pluckley, Kent. Second Edition.
18mo. cloth, 1*s.* 6*d.*

—— The Cottage Library. Vol. I. The Sacra-
ment of Baptism. 18mo. sewed, 1*s.*; or cloth, 1*s.* 6*d.*

"A little book of probably large usefulness. It avoids disputed points, but conveys a
clear and simple view of the holy rite of baptism. It is admirably suited to the cottage,
as well as to all places in which ignorance reigns upon the subject."—*Church and State
Gazette.*

—— The Cottage Library. Vol. II. The Sacra-
ment of the Lord's Supper. Third Edition. 18mo. cloth, 1*s.*

OXENDEN, Rev. A.
—— The Cottage Library. Vol. III. A Plain
History of the Christian Church. Second Edition. 18mo. cloth, 1s.

—— The Cottage Library. Vol. V. God's Message
to the Poor: being Eleven Plain Sermons preached in Pluckley Church.
Second Edition. 18mo. cloth, 2s.

—— The Cottage Library. Vol. VI. The Story
of Ruth. 18mo. cloth, 2s.

OXFORD, Bishop of. —— Four Sermons, preached
before Her Most Gracious Majesty Queen Victoria in 1841 and 1842.
By SAMUEL, Lord Bishop of Oxford, Chancellor of the Most Noble Order
of the Garter, Lord High Almoner to the Queen. Published by Com-
mand. Third Edition. Fcap. 8vo. cloth, 4s.

PARKER, Miss F. S.——Truth without Novelty; or,
a Course of Scriptural Instruction for every Sunday in the Year, principally designed for Private Family Instruction and Sunday Schools.
By FRANCES S. PARKER. Second Edition. Fcap. cloth, 3s.

PARRY, Sir W. E. —— Thoughts on the Parental
Character of God. By Rear-Admiral Sir WILLIAM EDWARD PARRY, R.N.
late Lieut.-Governor of Greenwich Hospital. Fifth Edition. 18mo.
cloth, 1s. 6d.

PEARS, Rev. S. A.——Over the Sea; or, Letters
from an Officer in India to his Children at Home. Edited by the Rev.
S. A. PEARS, D.D. Head-Master of Repton School. Fcap. cloth, with
Illustrations. 4s. 6d.

"These letters from 'Over the Sea' contain just the kind of information that one
wishes to have about the country and the people of India, and the mode of life of the
English in the East. The description of scenery and sketches of native character and
customs are graphic and entertaining, and the pictures are all the more vivid from the
style being such as was deemed most adapted for youthful readers."—*Literary Gazette.*

". . . their tone is so manly, sensible, and affectionate, with a pervading element of
unobtrusive religious principle, that it is impossible to read them without a feeling of
regard for the anonymous writer, and interest in his youthful correspondents."—
Guardian.

"These letters possess two valuable qualities—reality and simplicity."—*Record.*

—— Three Lectures on Education. 18mo. cloth,
1s.

"The position occupied by Dr. Pears ought to give authority to his remarks on
Education, and all that is contained in this little book is characterised by practical
wisdom."— CLERICAL JOURNAL.

"We recommend this little book to the notice of every teacher and head of a family."
—THE BEACON.

PEARSON, Rev. J. N.—Sunday Readings for the
Family and the Closet. By the Rev. J. NORMAN PEARSON, M.A.
12mo. cloth, 7s.

> "Sound and practical."—*British Magazine.*
> "A most valuable work."—*Church of England Magazine.*

—— The Days in Paradise, in Six Lectures.
12mo. cloth, 3s.

Peep of Day; or, a Series of the Earliest Religious
Instruction the Infant Mind is capable of receiving. With Verses
illustrative of the Subjects. Hundred and Fortieth Thousand, revised and corrected. 18mo. cloth, 2s.

—— Part II.; or, More about Jesus. By the same
Author. Fifteenth Thousand. 18mo. cloth, 2s. 6d.

Practical Suggestions towards Alleviating the Sufferings of the Sick. Part II. Fourth Edition. 12mo. cloth, 6s. 6d.

PRATT, Archdeacon.—Scripture and Science not
at Variance: with Remarks on the Historical Character, Plenary
Inspiration, and Surpassing Importance, of the Earlier Chapters of
Genesis. By JOHN H. PRATT, M.A., Archdeacon of Calcutta; Author
of the "Mathematical Principles of Mechanical Philosophy." Third
Edition, with Additions, 8vo. cloth, 3s. 6d.

> "This instructive essay . . . is admirably adapted for the designed end. The style is
> lucid and vigorous : the argument solid and convincing."—*Record.*
> "A very seasonable work."—*Church of England Magazine.*
> "Written with elegance, talent, and, still better, with a competent knowledge of the
> subject, and excellent judgment."—*Eclectic Review.*

PRAYERS, Family and Private.

A Form of Prayers, Selected and Composed for
the Use of a Family principally consisting of Young Persons.
Fifteenth Edition. 12mo. cloth, 2s. 6d.

A Manual of Family and Occasional Prayers.
By the Rev. WILLIAM SINCLAIR, M.A. 18mo. cloth, 1s. 6d.

PRAYERS, Family and Private.

A Selection of Prayers and Hymns. For the
Use of her Children. By the COUNTESS OF NORTHESK. In Two Parts,
12mo. 2s. cloth; or sewed, 1s.

Family Prayers. By the late HENRY THORN-
TON, Esq. M.P. Thirty-eighth Edition. 12mo. cloth, 3s.

Family Prayers for One Month. By various
Clergymen. Arranged and Edited by the Rev. CHARLES HODGSON,
M.A. Rector of Barton-le-Street, Yorkshire. Abridged Edition.
To which have been added, Prayers for Particular Seasons. Fcap.
cloth, 3s. 6d.

Seventy Prayers on Scriptural Subjects: being
a Selection of Scripture Daily Readings for a Year; with Family
Prayers for a Month. By Clergymen of the Church of England.
Fifth Ten Thousand. 12mo. cloth, 2s.

Family Prayers. By the late W. WILBERFORCE,
Esq. Edited by his Son. Eleventh Edition. Fcap. 8vo. sewed, 1s. 6d.

Family Prayers for Every Day of the Week.
Selected from various portions of the Holy Bible, with References.
Third Edition. 12mo. boards, 2s. 6d.

Family Prayers for Every Day in the Week.
By CLERICUS. 18mo. cloth, 1s.

Prayers and Offices of Devotion for Families
and for Particular Persons, upon most occasions. By BENJAMIN
JENKS. Altered and Improved by the Rev. CHARLES SIMEON. 12mo.
roan, 4s. 6d.; or 18mo. 3s.

A Course of Morning and Evening Prayers, for
the Use of the Families of the Poor. 12mo. sewed, 6d.; or 5s. per
dozen.

Private Prayers for Young Persons. By M. A.
Fcap. cloth, 2s.

PRAYERS, Family and Private.

A Few Plain Short Prayers, intended to be
sent with each set of Baby Linen lent to Poor Women. 24mo. sewed, 3*d.* ; or 2*s.* 6*d.* per dozen.

A Companion to the Altar, with Occasional
Prayers. By GEORGE A. E. MARSH, A.M. Rector of Bangor, Flintshire. Third Edition. Boards, 1*s.* 6*d.* ; sheep, 2*s.* ; calf, 3*s.*

Newly-Arranged Manual for Communicants at
the Lord's Supper, including the Service for the Holy Communion. 24mo. bound, 3*s.*

Prussian Oculist. A Manual of Information re-
specting the Ober Medicinal Rath de Leuw of Gräfrath. By An ENG-LISH CLERGYMAN. Second Edition, 18mo. cloth, 2*s.*

RAIKES, Rev. H.—Sermons and Essays. By the
Rev. HENRY RAIKES, late Chancellor of the Diocese of Chester. 8vo. cloth, 9*s.*

"It is needless to say that everything in the volume bears the impress of the author's mind and character. Sound evangelical doctrine is exhibited in elegant language, and illustrated from the resources of a cultivated understanding and a refined taste ; while the whole is pervaded with Christian toleration and sound good sense."—*Evangelical Christendom.*

RAWNSLEY, Rev. R. D. B.—Sermons Preached in
Country Churches. By R. DRUMMOND B. RAWNSLEY, M.A. Vicar of Shiplake, Oxon ; late Fellow of Magdalen College, Oxford. 12mo. cloth, 6*s.*

"A series of short, plain, and pithy sermons, adapted to the character and comprehension of a rural congregation."—*Spectator.*

"A good volume ; we can safely recommend it."—*St. James's Chronicle.*

—— Village Sermons. Second Series. 12mo.
5*s.* 6*d.*

"Enforces the practical duties of religion and the beauty of holiness."—*John Bull.*

"This is a volume of plain sermons in a simple unpretending style, adapted to the comprehension of the villagers to whom they are addressed, and inculcating many useful practical lessons."—*Church of England Magazine.*

—— Sermons, chiefly Catechetical. 12mo. cloth,
5*s.* 6*d.*

"Their plainness brings them within the comprehension of the most illiterate. whilst their exposition and illustration of Gospel truth render them a medium of usefulness, which cannot be without the very best results."—*Bell's Messenger.*

Reading without Tears; or, a Pleasant Mode of
Learning to Read. By the Author of "Peep of Day," &c. With numerous Woodcuts. New Edition. Square.

*** In this little work the attempt is made, by the *classification* of words, removing all perplexity, to prevent TEARS, and by a succession of *pictures*, furnishing constant entertainment, to preserve the SMILES of happy childhood while learning to read.

" That this elementary volume is the work of the authoress of the 'Peep of Day' will be a sure passport to the hearts of thousands, both parents and children. But apart from its authorship, the book itself is admirable ; the arrangement, pictures, typography, and reading exercises being alike adapted to realise the idea of the title, learning to read 'without tears.' Teachers are addressed in some valuable prefatory remarks. The authoress lays great stress on the exclusion of the element of fiction from the narratives which she has introduced as lessons."—*Record.*

The Rector in Search of a Curate. Post 8vo.
cloth, 9s.

Contents.—1. The Parish—2. The Curate—3. The Temporary Curate—4, 5. The Evangelicist—6. The Evangelicals—7. The Unfortunate Man—8. The Scholar—9. The Millenarian—10. The Anglo-Catholic—11. The Approved—12. The Ordination.

"A lively and entertaining book."—*Christian Observer.*
"Interesting and attractive."—*Spectator.*

RIPON, Bishop of.—Means of Grace. Lectures
delivered during Lent, 1851, in St. John's Church, Clapham Rise. By the Right Rev. ROBERT BICKERSTETH, D.D. Lord Bishop of Ripon. Fcap. cloth, 3s. 6d.

" Mr. Bickersteth's Lectures are very sterling in point of doctrinal teaching and practical enforcement."—*Christian Times.*
" These are plain, unaffected, and sensible discourses, setting forth the great outlines of Christianity and urging the necessity of holiness and obedience."—*English Review.*

RUPERT'S LAND, Bishop of.—Notes of the Flood
at the Red River, 1852. By DAVID ANDERSON, D.D. Lord Bishop of Rupert's Land. Fcap. cloth, 2s. 6d.

RUSSELL, Dr.—The History of Modern Europe.
With an Account of the Decline and Fall of the Roman Empire ; and a View of the Progress of Society, from the Rise of the Modern Kingdoms to the Peace of Paris in 1763. In a series of Letters from a Nobleman to his Son. New Edition, continued to the present time. 4 vols. 8vo. cloth, 2l. 12s.

Scenes in our Parish. By a Country Parson's
Daughter. 2 vols. 12mo. boards, each 5s.

SCOTT, Rev. T.— Essays on the most Important
Subjects in Religion. By the Rev. THOMAS SCOTT, late Rector of
Aston Sandford, Bucks. With a Memoir of the Author. Fifteenth
Edition. 12mo. 5*s.*; 18mo. 3*s.* 6*d.*

Scripture Catechism; extracted chiefly from the
Rev. Edward Bickersteth's " Scripture Help." Designed to assist the
Young in acquiring a Knowledge of the Holy Bible, and to commend it
to their love. By E. W. 18mo. 1*s.* sewed; 1*s.* 6*d.* cloth.

Sermons and Extracts Consolatory on the Loss of
Friends. Selected from the Works of the most eminent Divines.
Third Edition. 8vo. cloth, 12*s.*

SHAKSPEARE.—The Plays of William Shakspeare,
accurately printed from the Text of the Corrected Copies, a History of
the Stage, and a Life of Shakspeare. By ALEXANDER CHALMERS, F.S.A.
8 vols. 8vo. 3*l.* 12*s.*; or 1 vol. 8vo. 10*s.* 6*d.*

SHERWOOD, Mrs.—The Golden Garland of Inesti-
mable Delights. By Mrs. SHERWOOD. 12mo. cloth, 6*s.*

" It possesses greater reality, and even interest, than some more ambitious-looking
tales ; everything in ' the Golden Garland ' bears the stamp of truth."—*Spectator.*
" It serves as a vehicle to inculcate the soundest moral precepts," &c.—*Herald.*

—— The Mirror of Maidens in the Days of Good
Queen Bess. 12mo. cloth, 6*s.*

—— The History of John Marten. A Sequel to
" The Life of Henry Milner." 12mo. cloth, 7*s.* 6*d.*

—— The History of Henry Milner. 3 vols. 12mo.
cloth, each 6*s.*

—— The History of the Fairchild Family; or,
The Child's Manual. Nineteenth Edition. 3 vols. 12mo. cloth, each 5*s.*

—— Julietta di Lavenza. A Tale. 18mo. cl. 2*s.*

—— Victoria. 12mo. boards, 4*s.*

—— The Little Momiere. 12mo. cloth, 2*s.*

SHIRLEY, Bishop.—Letters and Memoir of the late WALTER AUGUSTUS SHIRLEY, D.D. Lord Bishop of Sodor and Man. Edited by THOMAS HILL, B.D. Archdeacon of Derby. Second Edition, revised. With a Portrait, 8vo. cloth, 14s.

—— Letters to Young People. By the late Right Rev. WALTER AUGUSTUS, Bishop of Sodor and Man. Fcap. cloth, 3s. 6d.

"The volume consists of letters chiefly addressed to his son and daughter ; and exhibits the writer in a very amiable, affectionate, pious, and sensible light. Some of the epistles to his son contain judicious advice on study and critical remarks on books."—*Spectator.*

"We like the general tone of these letters much. They are cheerful, unaffected, kindly, without overweening conceit or laborious condescension. They refer, too, to real incidents and events."—*Athenæum.*

—— Sermons preached on Various Occasions. 12mo. cloth, 6s.

"A direct plainness of style and purpose, which had the effect of force, and a sound Protestant feeling."—*Spectator.*

SIMEON, Rev. C.—Memoirs of the Rev. CHARLES SIMEON, M.A. late Senior Fellow of King's College, and Minister of Trinity Church, Cambridge ; containing his Autobiography, together with Selections from his Writings and Correspondence. Edited by the Rev. WILLIAM CARUS, M.A. Canon of Winchester. Third Edition. 12mo. cloth, with Portrait and Facsimile, 5s.

SMITH, Rev. J. H.—Sermons by JOHN HENRY SMITH, M.A. Perpetual Curate of Milverton, Warwickshire. Second Edition, with additions. 2 vols. 12mo. cloth, 12s.

"The subjects are commonplace and practical, such as 'The Gospel Invitation,' 'Christ's Invitation to the Heavy-laden,' 'Our Saviour's Love of Solitude.' &c. ; but there is a tender and earnest spirit displayed in the treatment of them, which of itself would secure attention. And there is also a vivacity and power of illustration in the style, which still more would gain the attention of the hearer."—*Clerical Journal.*

"Mr. Smith's sermons remind us of some of the best discourses of Melville. There is the same habit of seizing upon some one truth in the text, bringing it out into new and interesting combinations, throwing the discussion into an argumentative mould, and ringing out the idea in the music of lofty language. These sermons have life in them, and they will live and generate living thoughts in thoughtful readers. Every sermon bespeaks independency of research, vigour of intellect, and a reverent, catholic, manly Christianity."—*The Homilist.*

SMITH, Rev. T. D. S.—Life : an Enquiry into the Source, Actings, and Results of the Divine or Spiritual Life. By the Rev. THOS. D. S. SMITH, B.A. Curate of Bishopstoke. Crown 8vo. cloth, 6s.

SMITH, Rev. W. M.—Help to District Visitors. Being Plain and Practical Remarks on some Portions of the Gospels; particularly the Narratives and Parables. With an Appendix of Prayers selected from the Liturgy. By the Rev. W. MAXWELL SMITH, Rector of Lufton, and Perpetual Curate of Tintinhull, Somersetshire. Fcap. 8vo. cloth, 3s. 6d.

"Plain, scriptural. and affectionate, it cannot fail to do good,"whether read by those that visit the poor, or placed in village or parochial libraries."—CLERICAL JOURNAL.

"The pieces are short, sensible, and scriptural."—CHURCH OF ENGLAND MAGAZINE.

"These addresses are models of their kind."—MORNING HERALD.

"Many important topics are herein brought home to the simplest mind. The district visitor cannot do better than provide himself with the work."—BEACON.

"We shall be glad to hear that Mr. Smith's valuable work has a large circulation."—WESTERN FLYING POST.

Solace of a Mourner. Fcap. cloth, 4s. 6d.

STEPHEN, Sir G.—Anti-Slavery Recollections: in a Series of Letters addressed to Mrs. BEECHER STOWE. Written by Sir GEORGE STEPHEN, at her Request. Fcap. cloth, 4s.

STEWART, Rev. J. H.—Memoir of the Life of the Rev. James Haldane Stewart, M.A. late Rector of Limpsfield, Surrey. By his Son, the Rev. DAVID DALE STEWART, M.A. Incumbent of All Saints', Maidstone. With a Portrait. Second Edition. 12mo. cloth, 5s.

—— The Family which Jesus Loved; or the History of Martha, and Mary, and Lazarus. In Seventeen Lectures. By the late Rev. J. H. STEWART. Third Edition. Fcap. cloth, 5s.

STOKES, Rev. E.—Sermons by Edward Stokes, M.A. Student of Christ Church, Rector of Staines, late Whitehall Preacher, and Select Preacher in the University of Oxford. Fcap. cloth, 5s. 6d.

"One great advantage of English sermons over those of most foreign preachers—we speak of good specimens of either class—is, that the former will bear reading as well as hearing. Those now before us, by Mr. Stokes, illustrate this good quality ; they do not deal with any controverted subject, and very little with doctrine at all; but there is a tone of real piety and of love towards Christ pervading them, which stamp them as essentially Christian sermons."—*Literary Churchman.*

STOWELL, Rev. H.—Tractarianism Tested by Holy Scripture and the Church of England, in a Series of Sermons. By HUGH STOWELL, M.A. Incumbent of Christ Church, Salford, Honorary Canon of Chester, and Rural Dean. 2 vols. 12mo. cloth, each 6s.

N.B. The object of this work is not merely nor mainly to confute Tractarianism, but rather to inform and establish the minds of Churchmen on certain perplexing questions, respecting which definite views are much needed.

STOWELL, Rev. H.

——— A Model for Men of Business; or, Lectures on the Character of Nehemiah. Third Edition. Crown 8vo. cloth, 5*s.*

THORNTON, H.—Female Characters. By the late HENRY THORNTON, Esq. M.P. With Prayers adapted to the Lectures. Second Edition. Fcap. cloth, 3*s.*

——— Family Commentary on Portions of the Pentateuch; in Lectures, with Prayers adapted to the Subjects. Second Edition. Thick 8vo. cloth, 12*s.*

——— On the Ten Commandments, with Prayers. Second Edition. 12mo. cloth, 2*s.* 6*d.*

——— Family Prayers, in a Series for a Month. Thirty-eighth Edition. 12mo. cloth, 3*s.*

——— Family Commentary upon the Sermon on the Mount. Second Edition. Fcap. cloth, 3*s.*

TRACTS for Distribution.

The Angel's Message; or, the Saviour made known to the Cottager. By the Author of "Peep of Day." Third Thousand. Square 16mo. price 6*d.*

By the same Author,

Teaching Myself; or, an Abridgment of "Reading without Tears." For the Cottager in his own Home. Fourth Thousand. Square 16mo. price 4*d.*

Tracts for Children; or, Fifty-two Facts from the Bible for the Fifty-two Sundays of the Year. Thirteenth Thousand. In a packet of Fifty-two Tracts; or, bound together in a volume, cloth gilt, price 2*s.*

TRACTS for Distribution.

The German Tree.   A Moral for the Young.
By the Rev. T. GOODWIN HATCHARD, M.A. Rector of Havant;
Domestic Chaplain to the Marquis Conyngham.   1*s.*

By the same Author,

Feed My Lambs.   A Lecture for Children in
Words of One Syllable; to which is added a Hymn.   Seventh Thousand.   32mo. 3*d.*; or 2*s.* 6*d.* per dozen.

My Duty.   The Christian Duties, taken from
the Church Catechism, printed in red and black within an ornamental Gothic Tablet; intended for Parochial Distribution.   4*d.*
each; or 3*s.* 6*d.* per dozen.

The Fourth Commandment Explained.   By a
Sunday-School Teacher.   3*d.*; or 2*s.* 6*d.* a dozen.

The Teacher's Assistant in Needle-work.   6*d.*
each, or 5*s.* per dozen.

The Knitting-Teacher's Assistant.   6*d.*; or 5*s.*
per dozen.

A Misfortune Changed into a Blessing.   12mo.
6*d.*; or 1*s.* cloth.

Eliezer; or, The Faithful Servant.   12mo. 3*d.*;
or 2*s.* 6*d.* per dozen.

How can I go to Church? or, a Dialogue
between a Lady and a Poor Woman.   3*d.* each.

Why should I not go to the Meeting-House?
3*d.* each.

Seed-Time and Harvest.   Some Account of
" Schools for the Destitute."   By the Author of " The Gospel of
Other Days."   Third Edition.   6*d.*

TRACTS for Distribution.

A Friend to the Sick and Afflicted. 3*d.*; or
2*s.* 6*d.* per dozen.

Thoughts on the Sabbath. 12mo. 3*d.*

Reflections on the Sabbath. By Sir HENRY
DYMOKE. 12mo. 3*d.*

Repairing the Church. 3*d.*; or 2*s.* 6*d.* per doz.

Narrative of Poll Peg, of Leicestershire. 3*d.*;
or 2*s.* 6*d.* per dozen.

The Curate Catechising; or, an Exposition of
the Church Catechism. By the Rev. W. THISTLETHWAITE, A.M.
Sixth Edition. 18mo. 1*s.*

By the same Author,

The Church Communicating; or, an Exposition
of the Communion Service of the Church of England. 18mo. 6*d.*

The Parochial Minister's Letter to the Young
People of his Charge on Confirmation. By the Rev. JOHN LANG-
LEY, Rector of St. Mary's, Wallingford. 12mo. 2*s.* per dozen.

A Short Catechism; or, Plain Instruction, containing the Sum of Christian Learning, set forth by the authority
of his Majesty, King Edward the Sixth, for all Schoolmasters to
Teach, A.D. 1553. 18mo. 6*d.*; or 5*s.* per dozen.

Confirmation: its Nature, Importance, and Be-
nefits. By the Rev. T. GRIFFITH, A.M. 4*d.*; or 3*s.* 6*d.* per dozen.

A Plain and Affectionate Address to Young
Persons about to be Confirmed. By the Right Rev. D. WILSON,
late Lord Bishop of Calcutta. 12mo. 4*d.*

By the same Author,

A Plain and Affectionate Address to Young
Persons, previously to Receiving the Lord's Supper. 12mo. 4*s.*

TUPPER, M. F.—Proverbial Philosophy. By MARTIN F. TUPPER, D.C.L. &c. Post 8vo. cloth, with Portrait, 8s.

—— An Illustrated Edition of Proverbial Philosophy.

THE DESIGNS BY

C. W. Cope, R.A.	John Gilbert.
Fred. R. Pickersgill, A.R.A.	James Godwin.
John Tenniel.	William Harvey.
Edward H. Corbould.	J. C. Horsley.
George Dodgson.	William L. Leitch.
Edward Duncan.	Joseph Severn.
Birket Foster.	Walter Severn.

The Ornamental Initials and Vignettes by Henry Noel Humphreys.

In 4to. bound in cloth, gilt edges, 21s.; morocco extra by Hayday, 36s.

—— The Pocket Edition of Proverbial Philosophy. Thirty-fourth. 16mo. cloth, gilt leaves, 5s.

—— Probabilities: an Aid to Faith. Third Edition. Fcap. cloth, 4s.

"It is difficult to convey, by extracts, the charm which is diffused over this little book. There is, in the infinite variety of subject, a continuous line of thought, which fixes the attention to its progress, and leaves the mind amused and edified with the perusal."—*Christian Remembrancer.*

TYTLER, Miss A. F.—Leila; or, the Island. Eighth Edition. Fcap. 8vo. cloth, 4s. 6d.

—— Leila in England. A Continuation of "Leila; or, the Island." Sixth Edition. Fcap. cloth, 6s.

—— Leila at Home; a Continuation of "Leila in England." By ANN FRASER TYTLER. Fourth Edition. Fcap. 8vo. cloth, 4s. 6d.

"'Leila at Home,' in continuation of 'Leila in England,' is written in the same pleasant style, and conveys similar lessons of an instructive and religious tendency."—*Literary Gazette.*

—— Mary and Florence; or, Grave and Gay. Eleventh Edition. Fcap. cloth, 4s. 6d.

TYTLER, Miss A. F.

—— Mary and Florence at Sixteen. Fifth Edition.
Fcap. cloth, 6s.

"These works are excellent. Miss Tytler's writings are especially valuable for their religious spirit. She has taken a just position between the Rationalism of the last generation and the Puritanism of the present, while the perfect nature and true art with which she sketches from juvenile life, show powers which might be more ambitiously displayed, but cannot be better bestowed."—*Quarterly Review.*

TYTLER, Miss M. F.—The Wooden Walls of Old
England: or, Lives of Celebrated Admirals. By Margaret Fraser Tytler. Containing Biographies of Lord Rodney, Earls Howe and St. Vincent, Lords de Saumarez and Collingwood, Sir Sydney Smith and Viscount Exmouth. Fcap. cloth, 5s.

—— Tales of the Great and Brave. Containing
Memoirs of Wallace, Bruce, the Black Prince, Joan of Arc, Richard Cœur de Lion, Prince Charles Edward Stuart, Nelson, and Napoleon Bonaparte. Second Edition. Fcap. cloth, 5s.

VENN, Rev. H.—Memoir and Selection from the
Correspondence of the Rev. H. Venn, M.A. Edited by the Rev. Henry Venn, B.D. Prebendary of St. Paul's. Seventh Edition. Fcap. cloth, 7s.

Verschoyle. A Roman Catholic Tale of the Nineteenth Century. 12mo. cloth, 6s.

VICTORIA, Bishop of.— Lewchew and the Lew-
chewans; being a Narrative of a Visit to Lewchew, or Loo-Choo, in October, 1850. By George Smith, D.D. Bishop of Victoria. Fcap. cloth, 2s. 6d.

—— Hints for the Times; or, the Religions of
Sentiment, of Form, and of Feeling, contrasted with Vital Godliness. Fcap. sewed, 1s. 6d.

"A sensible and seasonable little treatise."—*Christian Guardian.*

WEBB, Mrs. J. B.—The Beloved Disciple. Reflec-
tions on the History of St. John. By Mrs. J. B. Webb, Author of "Naomi," "Reflections on the History of Noah," &c. Fcap. 8vo. cloth, 4s. 6d.

"Very sensible and well-written reflections on the History of St. John. We can safely recommend it."—*Christian Guardian.*

WHITE, Rev. G.—The Natural History and Antiquities of Selborne. By the Rev. GILBERT WHITE, M.A. A New Edition, with Notes, by EDWARD TURNER BENNETT, Esq. F.L.S. &c. 8vo. cloth, 18*s.*

WILLYAMS, Miss J. L.—Chillon; or, Protestants of the Sixteenth Century. An Historical Tale. By JANE LOUISA WILLYAMS. 2 vols. 8vo. cloth, 10*s.*

"We think highly of this pathetic story. A true spirit of cheerful piety pervades its pages ; the characters are nicely discriminated, and many of the scenes are very vividly portrayed. All who read it may derive benefit from its perusal."—*Britannia.*

WOLFE, Rev. C.—Six Plain Sermons, preached to a Rural Congregation. By the Rev. CHARLES WOLFE, late Curate of Kemsing, Kent. Fcap. cloth, 2*s.* 6*d.*

WOODWARD, Rev. H.—Short Readings for Family Prayers, Essays, and Sermons. By the Rev. HENRY WOODWARD, A.M., formerly of Corpus Christi College, Oxford; Rector of Fethard, in the Diocese of Cashel. 8vo. cloth, 12*s.*

Words of Wisdom for my Child; being a Text for Every Day in the Year, for the use of very Young Children. Second Edition. 32mo. cloth, 2*s.*

YORKE, Rev. C. J.—Original Researches in the Word of God. By the Rev. C. J. YORKE, M.A. Rector of Shenfield. Fcap. cloth, 5*s.*

      I. Christ Known before His Advent.
     II. The Beauty of the Mosaic Law.
    III. Inspiration and Genius.
    IV. The Divine Recognition of the Spiritual Church.
     V. The Development of Pure Religion.
    VI. The Apostolic Motive.
   VII. God Apparent in His Miracles and Prophecies.
  VIII. Scriptural Imagery: its Uses, Marks, and Sources.
    IX. God Traced in the World, and Found in Christ.
     X. The Human Conscience.